Crossing Lines

Cleveland Clash 2

ELLEY ARDEN

author of *Heal My Heart* and *Running Interference*

CRIMSON ROMANCE
F+W Media, Inc.

Published by
Crimson Romance
an imprint of F+W Media, Inc.
10151 Carver Road, Suite 200
Blue Ash, OH 45242. U.S.A.
www.crimsonromance.com

ISBN 10: 1-4405-8249-1
ISBN 13: 978-1-4405-8249-3
eISBN 10: 1-4405-8248-3
eISBN 13: 978-1-4405-8248-6

This is a work of fiction. Names, characters, corporations, institutions, organizations, events, or locales in this novel are either the product of the author's imagination or, if real, used fictitiously. The resemblance of any character to actual persons (living or dead) is entirely coincidental.

Cover art © iStockphoto.com/cbarnesphotography

*To my husband, who loves order but deals
with my chaos because he loves me more.*

Acknowledgments

Life does not stop for deadlines, a fact I learned while simultaneously writing this book and dealing with some health issues. (Nothing serious, thank goodness!) As a result, this book would not have been possible without a serious group effort. To my editor, Tara Gelsomino, who is patient and kind and pushes me across the line book after book: I respect you more than you will ever know. To my mom and dad, who came all the way from Florida and cleaned my house, cooked my food, and made sure the laundry was clean: There is no physical or emotional pain that seeing your smiling faces can't fix. To my eighteen-year-old son, who drove carpool for his younger siblings so I could write "a few more words": I'm going to miss your steadfast support and easy smile next year when you're off conquering your dreams. To Danielle Barclay and Nicole Prebeck at Barclay Publicity, who plotted and planned behind the scenes while I toiled away: You helped me breathe easier. To Nichole D., whose effervescence blasts through the computer screen: Your story reminds me of how amazing and unstoppable female athletes truly are. To former Marine Chris C., who answered my shower questions quickly and seriously, and to his wife, Georgia, who didn't kill me for asking those questions in the first place: You made me laugh, and that's a huge thing! Life isn't always easy. Adding deadlines to it makes it downright crazy. But it's a crazy I'm honored to have, and I thank you all for the part you've played in it.

Chapter One

Jillian Bell flipped down the visor on her rusted Volvo wagon and assessed the damage on her face. Dark circles or caked mascara from the night before, bloodshot eyes, and hair like something from a static-cling science experiment. *Yikes.* She was a complete mess. Thankfully, it was all fixable.

She reached into the glove box that doubled as her "band promoter Rx kit." No party-girl-by-night and football-player-by-day could live without eye drops, baby wipes, hair ties, and chewing gum. Under a mess of fast-food napkins, crinkled promo flyers, Advil, condoms, guitar picks, hard candy, and cigarette lighters, she found the essentials that would deem her passable enough to keep Coach Howl off her ass.

One energy drink and three sticks of spicy cinnamon gum later, Jillian climbed out of her car and headed for the locker room. *No harm, no foul.*

"Oh my God!" Jade Wren, Jillian's new roommate and the Clash's starting center, pounced the minute Jillian walked into the locker room. "Where the heck have you been for the past two days? I thought something bad happened to you!"

"I was out having fun, and fun is never bad," Jillian said with a smile.

"It is when it makes you late." Tanya Martin, offensive linewoman and Jillian's ex-roommate, made a face and then pushed past Jillian and out the door.

Did she say late? Jillian looked at her phone. "What are you talking about? It's only 5:37. Practice doesn't start until 6:00."

MJ Rooney, the quarterback, shook her head. "Wrong. Coach e-mailed on Saturday night to say we're starting fifteen minutes early today." MJ followed Tanya out of the locker room.

Well, that sucked. Jillian didn't remember much about Saturday night, and she hadn't checked her e-mails in days. "It's okay." She flashed a cocky grin at Jade. "I still have…" she looked at her phone again, "six minutes. I'll be out there before anybody misses me."

As the locker room emptied out, Jillian flew through her prepractice ritual, skipping the usual taping of her ankles and bopping around to Eminem's "Lose Yourself." Everything was going beautifully, until she reached inside her duffle bag for her cleats. They weren't there.

"Shit!" Where could they be? *The trunk*. She'd tossed them back there after Saturday's game because they were muddy. Without a second thought, she sprinted to her car, and by the time she made it to the field, it was 5:47.

Oh well, at least she hadn't missed much. Her teammates were still huddled around Coach Howl. With any luck, her late arrival wouldn't even be noticed. She sidled up to Tanya and tried to look like she'd always been standing there.

"If anyone can explain to me what went wrong on Saturday, I'd love to hear it," Coach Howl said. But he didn't wait for anyone to speak up. He kept right on railing them over the fifty-four to seven loss.

What a drag. Jillian tried to tune him out. Her eyes skipped to the unfamiliar man standing behind Coach. *Daaaamn*. That man was fine. Fairly young, too. Thick, blond hair. Bold, blue eyes. Rugged face. And biceps that looked like they lifted small cars instead of weights. That was the kind of man that drew you in like a tractor beam and made you lick your lips in case you were drooling.

The gorgeous man took a few fluid steps and stopped beside Coach Howl.

"Who is *that*?" Tanya asked.

"Thor." Jillian said reverently. "And girl, I'd sell my soul to see his hammer."

Tanya chuckled.

Coach raised a hand above his head, signaling for everyone to quiet down. "Coach Malloy is no longer with us."

Wait! What? There were expressions of shock and murmurs all around her, but for once, Jillian was speechless. Coach Malloy was her "dude." He'd said they were kindred spirits, because they worked beautifully together, even sang everything from rock classics to eighties music during team stretches. He didn't rag on her for talking out of turn, showing off in the end zone, or running a little late. He was a blast, and when it came to football, they were on the exact same page. They'd made plans for this season. Big plans. They were going to prove a women's football team could run a wicked West Coast offense. And yeah, so the first three games—all losses—didn't have them off to a roaring start, but they still had time ... or so she'd thought.

"You fired him?!" She lifted her chin when Coach Howl shot her a death stare.

"He resigned," Coach said.

"*Bullshit,*" she coughed into her hand. Coach Malloy probably got the blame for the losses. It was no secret that this season, Coach Howl, who doubled as the running backs coach, wanted more emphasis on the running game.

Coach ignored her and moved on. "It's never easy to change coaches in the middle of a season, which means we have a lot of work to do. There will be several adjustments to make. Namely, I'd like to introduce you to your..."

At that exact moment, she remembered Thor. *Oh my God.* It couldn't be.

"... new offensive coordinator..."

It was.

"... and receivers coach ..."

Which meant Thor was "in charge" of her. Hot or not, she wasn't happy.

Jillian glance at her teammates to see how they were taking the news. Shocked faces all around.

"... Carter Howl, my son."

Oh no he didn't. Her head whipped around so fast she felt a sharp pain in her neck. Coach Howl replaced Coach Malloy with his son!

"You've got to be kidding me," she said a little too loudly, then grabbed her sore neck and rubbed. What was that bit about the apple not falling far from the tree? If that was true, then their passing game was doomed.

The younger Coach Howl looked at her, and—*ooh!*—those magic eyes produced a heat that pierced through her to the center of her neck pain, until she couldn't even feel her toes.

I'm cured, she thought, followed by, *maybe he won't be so bad*. In fact, maybe he wasn't anything like his father at all. Maybe he was the black sheep in his family—just like she was.

He looked away, patted his father on the shoulder, and then stepped up to address the team. "Ladies, I'm honored to be here," he said. "Rather than bore you with details about my football background, let me just say that I have plenty of experience with both the sport and the discipline needed to get the job done. Winning isn't rocket science. The team that wins works harder and longer than the losing team, and the team that wins knows how to stay out of trouble—on and off the field."

Why the hell was he looking at her?

She rolled her eyes. He narrowed his.

"*You* were late," he said.

She looked behind her, knowing full well he was talking to her. "Barely late."

At her response, he stood straighter and narrowed his eyes until they were slits. "Late is late, and it's not tolerated on this field." He made a whirling signal with his finger. "Laps ... until I tell you to stop."

He had to be kidding. She was the best player on this team. She'd scored every single one of the twenty-one points they'd scored so far this season.

She crossed her arms and looked at Coach Howl. He was no help. The faintest smile curved his lips.

"I miss Coach Malloy already!" she yelled as she threw her helmet to the sidelines and started jogging around the track.

By the time Thor deigned to release her from lap running, stretching was over and her mood was foul. She got in line and readied to run routes.

"Partying got the best of you this weekend, didn't it?" MJ asked.

"Never." They just had a new OC with a stick up his ass. Or a hammer. She looked at him and snickered.

He paced the sidelines, watching the team's every move, looking way too serious for his own good. *He's going to have a heart attack*, she thought. Which wouldn't be terrible. At least then he couldn't coach anymore.

He stopped pacing and stood with his feet shoulder width apart, a position that showed off strong thigh muscles beneath his thin athletic pants. She bet he had a six-pack. What a shame. God had formed a whole lot of fine man around one big asshole.

"Second group!" Coach yelled. "Slant. I want to see the head tilt."

Jillian stepped up to the line and got into her stance. The instant the whistle blew, everything else faded away.

A couple hours later, she was sweaty and exhausted, and that made everything else tolerable.

"Bell!"

Oh hell. Thor's voice boomed above the noisy chatter of her teammates, who were stampeding toward the locker room. She pretended like she didn't hear him.

"Bell, I know you can hear me."

What was with this guy? She stopped but didn't give him the satisfaction of turning around.

"You were five minutes late today, so tomorrow you will be fifteen minutes early."

Which didn't make any sense. She spun around. "I already paid my debt by running laps."

"Your debt will be paid when I say it's been paid. Fifteen minutes before everyone else. Right here." He pointed to the field. "Or you'll give me fifteen minutes on the bench this Saturday. Your choice."

What a jerk!

When she reached the locker room, she threw her cleats into her locker with a satisfying bang.

"We're going out tonight," she said to Jade emphatically. She needed shots of Patrón and loud dance music to wash away the suck of dealing with Tweedledee and Tweedledum of the Gridiron. "You and you..." she pointed at Tanya and MJ, "are more than welcome if your balls..." she chuckled, "and chains give you permission." Both of them had moved out of her apartment and in with guys who took up way too much of their time. What a drag! Having to ask permission to go out? No thank you. Jillian hadn't answered to anyone since she'd left home at nineteen. And she liked it that way.

"Going out again isn't going to get the new OC off your back," MJ said.

She did not want to talk about Thor.

"Maybe you should stay in tonight," Jade said. "We could watch a movie."

"That's boring," Jillian said.

Tanya gave her a knowing look. "I think you could use some boring. You were late for practice, Jill. That's a big deal, even for you."

Her frustration peaked. "It was five minutes!" she yelled. "I've been twenty minutes late before and Malloy never batted an eyelash! Man, I can't believe Coach sacked him to give his own son a job. Nepotism is the fucking worst. I bet he's a shitty—"

"Your phone's ringing." Jade cut in on her rant, looking hesitant to even bring it up. She pointed at the white and silver iPhone vibrating on the bench. "See?"

Jillian saw the name Wendy Novick flash on the screen. "It's my sister," she said, and her stomach hollowed out. Two months ago, Wendy had given birth to her first child, a boy, who had been diagnosed with a congenital heart defect. Things weren't exactly good between Jillian and her family. She'd only seen her nephew via Facebook so far, and phone calls were rare. What if it was more bad news about Caleb?

"I should answer this," she said. MJ and Tanya were looking at her with concern.

Jillian wandered off in the direction of the training room where it was quiet. "Hello?"

"Hi. It's me ... Wendy."

"I know who it is, Wen. You're in my contacts. You show up on Caller ID." And even if she didn't, one word spoken in that sweet voice was all Jillian needed to recognize her little sister. "Is everything okay?" The words felt tacky on her tongue.

Wendy hesitated. "We're still waiting on an official date for his heart surgery." A long, heavy silence filled the line, and Jillian dropped into a nearby chair. "You're seeing the pictures I've been posting on Facebook, right?"

An image of her cute nephew popped into her head, and Jillian swallowed past the lump in her throat. "I am. He's a doll baby." He really was beautiful, and her sister looked so happy in all those photos. "I can't believe you're a mom now."

"I can't imagine not being a mom. I can't believe I ever *wasn't* a mom." Her soft chuckle was tinged with sadness.

"When are you supposed to hear about the surgery?"

"I don't know. This week, I hope. But, Jillie, you have to come meet him ... that's why I'm calling." Her sister paused. "I want you to come to his christening."

You could've knocked her over with a feather. "Seriously?"

"Yes, I want you to hold him before..." Wendy's voice cracked. "I don't know how long he will be in the hospital after the surgery, and I don't know how long it will be before people can hold him again. You want to meet him, don't you?"

"Of course I do." But the christening would probably be the social event of the year in Charity. The whole damn town would be there. Her parents, of course. Her jerk off of a brother-in-law, Bob. All those judgmental old church biddies and their redneck husbands. Not to mention the right Reverend G. Keller Winters, Jillian's ex-fiancé. She made a face. "Why don't I just come in for a quiet visit another time?"

"Please." Wendy's voice shook. "We hired a photographer. I'm going to scrapbook the whole thing. I want you to be there. I want Caleb to look back at these books someday and see you were there."

Oh God, her sister was crying. For a fleeting moment, Jillian was thrown back fifteen years to when their father was deployed with the Army, and Wendy cried herself to sleep every night he was gone. Just how risky would this surgery be? Considering how small the kid was, probably pretty damn risky. She should go, for Wendy and the baby, despite everyone else.

But it wasn't that simple.

"I'm in the middle of a rough football season." If Thor got his panties in a bunch over her missing five minutes of practice, what would he do if she missed a game?

"I know, but I was hoping you could work something out. Charity is only two hours from Cleveland. And he's being baptized on a Sunday. Surely you don't play on the Lord's Day. I mean, I would love for you to be here for everything. The layette breakfast is on Saturday morning. But I understand if you can only make it to the church on Sunday and the luncheon afterward. I'll take what I can get." Wendy's exhale echoed on the other end. "I want you there, Jillie. I *need* you there."

Wendy was quite possibly the only person in the world she had trouble saying no to, and under the circumstances, saying no would be a major jerk move. "Okay," she conceded. "I'll figure something out."

"Thank you. Thank you so much!"

Jillian felt a smile stretch across her face.

"Just promise me you'll tone it down," Wendy continued. "No alcohol this time. No cursing. Cover the tattoos. Please."

Jillian's muscles tensed. There was always a catch. But this time, how could she say no? After a long exhale, she said, "I'll give it a shot ... for you."

When the call ended, she wandered into the locker room.

"What's wrong?" Tanya asked immediately.

"Nothing's wrong." She put the phone on the top shelf of her locker and grabbed her towel off the hook.

"Liar. I can tell by your face."

"Nothing's wrong-wrong. Wendy wants me at Caleb's christening."

"That's good! It's an olive branch. Girl, you're an aunt. Embrace that, and kick the rest of the crap aside."

She wished she could, but going back to Charity was like walking through a land mine. She hated it! So much she could count on one hand the number of times she'd been back in the last seven years.

"Are you going to go?" MJ asked. The crinkled look on her face said she knew Jillian would at least try to get out of it.

"I feel like I have to. I mean he's sick. I should've seen him already." God, what kind of aunt did that make her? A shitty one, that was for sure.

"When is it?" Jade asked.

"Two weeks. It's a home game, so I could technically drive to Charity Saturday evening and then come home Sunday night. I wouldn't miss any football that way."

"That sounds great!" Jade smiled. Of course she did. She didn't know the whole story.

"It *would be* great if Bob wasn't there." Jillian exchanged glances with Tanya and MJ, because they knew exactly what she was talking about.

"Who's Bob?" Jade asked.

"Bob is Wendy's husband, and he hates me."

"For good reason," MJ added.

Jillian rolled her eyes. "Maybe."

Tanya laughed. "Definitely."

"Why does he hate you?" Jade was on the edge of the bench.

"I brought alcohol to the wedding, and I shared it with the best man, Bob's brother."

Jade looked confused. "Okay. What's wrong with that? Everybody drinks at weddings."

MJ sat beside Jade. "Charity is a dry town. No booze anywhere. Not even at weddings."

Jade grimaced.

"I know, right?" Jillian asked. "I just wanted to have fun. I mean my ex was the officiant. I had to stand through an entire ceremony listening to him talk about how a woman's place is subservient to her husband, who is her lord on earth." She pawed at her neck. "It made my skin crawl, but I respected Wendy, and I behaved…" she paused at a look from MJ, "until the reception. I couldn't stand another minute of all those self-righteous townies judging me. I had to let off a little steam." And through the years, Bruce had always been willing to let loose with her.

"I'm not sure you *had to* have sex with the best man in a broom closet." Tanya's head bobbed with attitude.

"Bob found them," MJ said, filling in the torrid conclusion for Jade. "He opened the door and got a fine shot of his little brother's ass."

Jade gasped. The other two laughed, having heard the story at least a dozen times.

Jillian smacked a hand to her forehead and rubbed it across her face. "I was drunk."

The icing on the whole bitter cake had been her parents throwing her out of the house the morning after. Going home for the first time since *that* was going to make this trip a million times harder.

"Wait a minute. Did I hear that right? Your ex is a priest?" Jade's eyes widened.

"A preacher," Jillian corrected. "But he wasn't a preacher when I was with him, and I wasn't..." she lifted a strand of electric blue hair, "like this. I was nineteen. It was a long time ago." Almost ten years. But she still didn't like seeing him, and she hated the judgment and pity in his eyes. She hated even more the town's collective opinion that she'd gone to hell after she'd turned down the love of a good man. Criticism like that made her do stupid things to prove that she was just fine the way she was.

"That's why Wendy wants me to clean up my act." Jillian cringed. "She said no drinking, no cursing, and cover up the tattoos." She looked down at the colorful collage climbing her right arm from wrist to elbow. "If it were anyone else asking me to do that, I'd tell them to go fuck themselves."

"Wait." Tanya gaped at her. "You mean to tell me you're going to do it? You're going to get rid of the blue streaks in your hair, wear long sleeves, and watch your mouth all weekend?"

"It's not *all* weekend. I'll be there less than forty-eight hours." Jillian ignored the tension in her chest. "I can manage it."

"I don't know why you would," MJ said. "It's not okay for them to ask you to be someone else simply to be good enough to meet your nephew."

Jillian sighed. "It's not like that ... at least, not for Wendy. She's fine with the way I am. She's just trying to protect me from the people who aren't."

MJ shook her head in disagreement. "I still don't like it."

"I still don't think you're capable of doing it," Tanya said.

Jillian glared at Jade. "You want to weigh in with some negativity, too? Make it unanimous?"

"Well..." Jade bit into her bottom lip. "It seems very stressful. I'm afraid you'll crack without serious support. Maybe one of us should go with you."

Ooh! She resented their lack of confidence. "I'll be fine," she said. In fact, better than fine. She would prove to them that she could be boring for one freaking weekend.

How hard could it be?

Chapter Two

Tuesday morning. 4:45 a.m.

Carter Howl didn't burn daylight.

He made his bed by the last remaining light of the moon streaming in through the floor-to-ceiling windows of his downtown Cleveland high-rise condo's master bedroom. He didn't need to turn on the lights. He got up this early every day. Weekends included. He could do this with his eyes closed.

Forty-five-degree-angle folds made up the mattress's corners. Exactly 14 inches of white sheet showed between the doubled-over bedding and the headboard. Pillows were centered on the white. Then he tucked the blankets beneath the mattress tightly on all sides. *Perfection.*

The only thing that had changed since his days in active duty was the bed size. His California king bed was like heaven on earth for a man who'd slept on the ground so many times he'd once considered sleeping on a cot beneath a behemoth logistics truck a luxury. A far cry from Egyptian-cotton sheets in a million-dollar condo with a view.

He walked to the wall of windows and watched the slowly rising sun turn the farthest edge of Lake Erie a ghostly yellow. He'd seen the sun rise in some pretty shitty corners of the world, which had taught him that a sunrise was always something to celebrate. Another day. Another opportunity to be better than you were the day before. *Seize that mother.*

He whistled for Hercules. The heavy gallop up the loft stairs announced the German shepherd's arrival even before Carter turned to see the dog barrel into the room.

He bent and roughed the hair between the dog's ears. "Ready?"

Like the dog did every morning, Hercules sprinted back downstairs to wait by the front door for their morning run. Enthusiasm within the confines of respect for the routine was a beautiful thing. Pairing his passion with his discipline had been the cornerstone for building his successful entertainment business. Just this year, Shock & Awe: American Bar, Grille & Games had been named the fastest-growing franchise in America. *Oorah!*

He grabbed his phone off the nightstand and his armband and earbuds out of the drawer. As he headed downstairs, he checked his e-mails.

A bunch of spam, urging him to log in to his bank account immediately or pop a pill for maximum sexual potency. He shook his head and deleted them. A few work e-mails he was expecting and would deal with at the office. And one from Michaela. The subject read: "I've been thinking …"

He stopped at the bottom of the stairs and read the message:

Carter,

I don't know how else to say this. It's not working for me, so I'm canceling out on Saturday. I know you're probably thinking I'm crazy, because you're handsome and successful, but there's just no spark, and it should be there by the third date. I'm sorry. I am. I was so hopeful it would work. Your car is amazing.

M

He'd been dumped by e-mail. But, hey, chin up, buddy, "Your car is amazing."

Are you fucking kidding me? This was not a great way to start the day.

He dissected that e-mail in his mind as he ran a three-mile route around his downtown West Lakeside neighborhood with Hercules by his side. Michaela had all the makings of being his type. Long hair, freckles, a CrossFit addiction, and a graduate degree. She was also ready to settle down, wanted kids, loved dogs, and was close with her family. Unfortunately, he couldn't argue with her comment about there being no spark. Their dates had fallen flat for him, too. The difference was, he'd been hopeful the spark would develop the more time they spent together.

"Left," he said, and Hercules made the turn without a single stutter in his rapid steps.

The e-mail nagged at him. What was he doing wrong when it came to women? Not that he couldn't get a woman. If all he wanted was sex, he could get that easily. He was in great shape. He'd been told lots of times he was good looking. And his car *was* amazing. But he wanted more than that. He was thirty now. His parents had married in their early twenties. His brother and sister, too. He was way behind the curve thanks to two tours in Iraq and a corporation that commandeered his life. And now, he could add the responsibilities of a football team to the mix.

But he hadn't been able to say no to an opportunity that put him back on the field with his dad. Carter's decision to quit college—and football—to enlist in the Marines had driven a wedge between him and his father that lingered to this day. Maybe this coaching gig would finally and completely close the gap.

"Halt." He slowed for a red light, and Hercules stopped, too.

Carter kept a bounce in his limbs as he waited for the light to turn and decided to stop obsessing. He'd find someone. Until then, he had Hercules.

The light turned green, and he said, "Go," before he stepped into the intersection and upped his pace. He hit a button on the side of his watch and lit up the face. This run wouldn't take more than twenty minutes. In a twenty-four-hour day, there wasn't a second to spare.

Afterward, he fed Hercules, showered, shaved, dressed for work, and then headed to the kitchen for his usual cheese omelet and coffee. Black.

At precisely 6:00 a.m., his front door opened and his best friend and co-worker, Cristian Chant, walked in.

"How was your commute?" Carter teased, making fun of the fact that their condos were only four doors apart.

"Grueling," Cris said with a laugh. "Nearly got hit head on by 8B, who refuses to look up from his damn phone when he's walking."

Carter smiled and slid a mug of coffee across the spotless black granite to the second barstool from the left end of the kitchen island, which had been Cris's preferred seat since they'd closed on nearly identical condos ten months ago.

Cris nodded a thank you. "How was your run?"

"Excellent. You know, you're welcome to join me anytime."

"Hell, no. I gave that psychotic fitness shit up the day I was honorably discharged." He patted his stomach. "As long as I can still see my toes, I figure I'm okay." He took a sip from his mug. "How 'bout football practice? How did that go?"

"Just like my father said it would. Rough. The receiver he warned me about walked in late and covered in attitude. She had a smart-ass answer for everything I said."

His father had given him the rundown on Bell, who was talented but distracted, confrontational, and potentially self-destructive. All of which had gotten progressively worse under Malloy's loose and divisive reign. All of which were expected to improve under Carter's regime.

"What'd you say? Did you tell her she throws like a girl?"

Carter made a face. "You wish you could throw like these girls." He cut the heat on the six-burner stove and slid the omelet onto his plate. "I made her run laps and then told her to come in fifteen minutes early tonight or I would bench her on Saturday. Tough love." He grinned.

"You're a bastard."

Carter laughed. "That's why my dad hired me—to do his dirty work. He'd rather spend his time drawing charts and thinking up new plays. Whatever. I'll be the heavy. At this point, I feel like I sort of owe him. Maybe we can get past this Marines thing once and for all. I mean it's not playing in the NFL like he wanted me to do, but it's still football."

Cris nodded. "Is anybody hot on the team?"

Again Carter made a face, but he found himself running through fuzzy images of the players in his mind. "I couldn't really tell because they're all in full equipment. Besides, that's the last thing I need to know. I'm not looking for a wife on that team. I'm looking for the standout athletes. I want to know how fast they are. How strong. Can they run a decent route? Can they catch? Those are more important questions."

"Who's hot is always the most important question to me."

"Because you're an ass." Carter took a bite of egg.

"No, I like ass. There's a difference. Ooh. Speaking of ass. I have a date with a yoga instructor Saturday night. You and Michaela want to double?"

He could've done without the reminder. That e-mail was more than a little blow to his ego. "I can't. She canceled."

"Okay. Then another time maybe."

"Probably not." Cris quirked an eyebrow. "We're moving on."

Cris shook his head. "You didn't even get to sleep with her."

Not that Carter had shared the details. Cris just knew him well enough to know about his rules for dating. Three full dates, at least a week apart, before he even thought about taking a woman to bed.

"There was no spark," he said.

"Because you don't go for spark. You have this crazy idea that you should be settling down and finding a wife, when you just need to relax and have fun. Thirty isn't old, man."

It felt old to him. Maybe that was because he'd grown up too fast, too soon thirteen years ago when his mother had died. He'd been seventeen and nowhere near ready to face the world without her guiding hand. Then came the Marines two years later, and the parts of him that hadn't grown up by then did so in a hurry. In the span of five years, he'd gone from a teen obsessed with football and video games to a man, fighting for his life and the lives of everyone around him. So many nights, he'd huddled scared in the dark, listening to Cris tell him they would get out alive. "Pretend it's a 3-D version of *Call of Duty*," Cris had said. And it had worked. It took the edge off the risk. In fact, the idea of video games as stress relievers took on a life of its own once Carter and Cris were stateside. *Damn.* It was still surreal to think a dream hatched on the battlefields of Afghanistan had become a rip-roaring reality.

"I'll tell you what you're going to do," Cris said. "You're going to go out there and do something crazy. Screw the schedules. Screw the rules. That's when you'll find the spark."

Something crazy, huh? "Like skydiving?"

"Sure, whatever floats your boat, but I was thinking more along the lines of something crazy involving a woman. Just something to get the adrenaline pumping."

Carter thought about it for a split second. It made some sense. He couldn't argue that he was in a rut, but doing something crazy often involved being unnecessarily careless. He didn't need crazy to turn into stupid, like gaining a stalker after a one-night stand. Besides, he had about all the crazy he could handle with coaching a full-tackle women's football team.

He washed the frying pan by hand, put the Corelle in the dishwasher, and polished the stainless steel cooktop. Cris watched him with an amused glint in his eyes.

"No, my domestic services are not for hire," Carter said.

"Thank God. You'd look like shit in a French maid outfit." They shared a laugh, but then Cris got serious. "I mean it, man.

You've got to break out of this rigid routine. It's not going to get you anywhere but an early grave."

Maybe. Maybe not. That rigid routine had gotten him here. He glanced around his luxury condo, then grabbed his leather satchel off a nearby chair, and pulled his keys from the front pocket. "I'll think about it."

That seemed to be enough to appease Cris, who smacked Carter on the shoulder and smiled. "If you need any advice along the way, I'm here. And if you want me to hook you up with something young and sweet, I got you covered, man."

Carter nodded. Then he held up his phone to capture what had become a daily picture of Hercules, who had assumed his usual 6:25 a.m. position on the couch.

Then he typed a quick message to his niece, Sophia:

Herky says he's the only one who's allowed to sleep in on weekdays, so get up, make your bed, get dressed, eat breakfast, and have a good day at school! Luv, Uncle Carter

"That's not normal, man," Cris said.

"What?"

"Taking pictures of your dog to send to your niece. It's just . . I don't know … it's old-man-like, and odd. Very odd."

"'Cause taking pictures of your junk to send to your yoga instructor isn't odd."

"I haven't junk-texted her … yet."

Carter trusted Cris with his life—just not with his social life. There was no way in hell he'd be taking that man's advice.

*

Showing up for practice fifteen minutes early ready to assume her "punishment"—a punishment she didn't entirely deserve—was one way to prove she could buckle down enough to survive two days in Charity. And just to drive the point home, Jillian showed up at the field a full thirty minutes early.

She pulled into the stadium parking lot feeling smug and in control. This was going to be a piece of cake.

I'm here

She group-texted Tanya, MJ, and Jade.

Way early, and I don't even resent it.

Well, not really. She snapped a smiling selfie as the ultimate proof.

She didn't expect immediate responses from Tanya and Jade, who were both teachers, wrapping up their days, but MJ's schedule was more flexible now that she was a dedicated motivational speaker.

MJ: I'm proud of you.
Jillian answered with a tongue-wagging emoji.

MJ: Just don't hurt our OC

Jillian: Bwahahahahaha! I could. Nobody else is here. I could tie him up and ...

Her fingers stilled, because damn it if she wasn't a little overheated at the image of Thor tied to her headboard. She finished off the sentence with

hurt him

Even though "lick him" was what rolled around in her head. She hit send with a lusty chuckle. But the lighthearted moment died the minute her phone vibrated and an incoming call from "Mom" lit up the screen.

Ignore it was Jillian's eternal initial thought where her mother was concerned, but considering she was trying to prove she could buck up and behave for Caleb's big day, didn't ignoring the call make her a chickenshit?

What to do? What to do? She tapped her fingers against the steering wheel. Technically she had thirteen minutes to burn. She could spend five talking to her mother, who hadn't called since the night Caleb had been born.

Jillian Bell, you are not a chickenshit. Answer the damn phone. She took a big breath and picked it up. Just another test to pass on her way home to Charity.

"Hello."

"Jillie." The pause was enough to rattle her. Who knew silence could be so judgmental? "Wendy says you're coming to the christening."

"I am." *Take that.* Anything that rattled the staunchly conservative woman had buoyed Jillian since she'd been thirteen.

"Well, then. I pray we won't have a repeat of what happened at the wedding."

It wasn't so much what she said but how she said it. That holier than thou voice had always pushed Jillian to the breaking point. "A repeat of what exactly?"

Her mother's haughty huff echoed. "I will not discuss your hedonistic behavior."

Ooh. Jillian sort of liked that word. There was nothing wrong with a little pleasure seeking. She grinned.

"I'll say this, though," her mother continued. "You embarrassed yourself and your family."

Oh, waah. "Everything would've been fine if Bob hadn't come sniffing around the broom closet. That guy's always looking for trouble."

"Bob was looking out for his brother!" Jillian rolled her eyes. "And he had reason to. You were making a scene all night. The drinking. The swearing. The vulgar dancing. The..."

And the list goes on. Jillian clenched her jaw. "Why don't you just say what you really mean—you can't stand any part of me! God, you're actually praying for me not to come home at all, aren't you?"

"Do not use the Lord's name in frustration."

Jillian bounced her head off the seat rest. "Whatever. I'm coming to the christening. Wendy wants me there, so I'll be there—whether anyone else likes it or not."

"If you ruin that baby's day, I'll never forgive you, Jillian Mae. He's had so much turmoil in his two short months, he deserves some joyful peace."

Jillian wouldn't argue with that.

Second thoughts slipped in. Maybe she shouldn't go. Maybe Tanya and MJ were right, and she was categorically unable to behave in stressful situations like going home to Charity. The weight of the decision gave her a rip-roaring headache. But even through the pain, she knew if she didn't go, she would disappoint Wendy, and in all honestly, she'd disappoint herself.

Jillian didn't back down from a challenge.

"I'm not going to ruin anything," she said emphatically.

Silence stretched out between them, and then her mother said, "I'll be praying for that."

But not for me, Jillian thought. She hated that it made her sad.

The call ended as stilted as it began, and Jillian decided she needed a few minutes to decompress before she took the field. She connected her iPhone to the stereo system and cranked up Fall Out Boy. Dropping her head to the seatback, she closed her eyes and wished there was a way to guarantee she would be on her best behavior in Charity. Maybe taking one of her friends wasn't such a bad idea. Then she would have someone who could kick her under the table if her lips got too loose, and she would have someone to bitch to when nobody else was around.

But it couldn't be Tanya, who was African American, or Jade, who was Korean American, because her parents were notoriously close-minded and unconsciously racist. Although a brief daydream of walking into Charity with them, arms linked and looking like an ad for the United Nations, made her smile. Her tattoos wouldn't be the biggest problem then. But Jillian wouldn't subject Tanya and Jade to that crap. No way.

That left MJ, who had already weighed in on what she thought about Jillian changing to gain other people's approval. She wasn't going to love the idea of toeing the line even for a weekend. Besides, if Jillian admitted to any of them that she wanted help getting through the weekend, she'd be admitting she couldn't do boring and righteous on her own. What a joke! She could do anything she put her mind to.

Still, the idea of taking someone stuck. There had to be one neutral person she could convince to come to Charity, someone who would keep her focused and make the whole thing easier. She thought of everyone she knew well enough to call in a favor, but they were band members, bar owners, college roommates, brothers and sisters of friends, exes, and teammates, who were just as likely to get drunk with her as they were likely to pull her away from a fight. Something like that could backfire big time. No, she didn't need a coconspirator; she needed a behavior coach. An unwelcomed image of Thor popped into her head.

Hell no! She did not need a drill sergeant to get through a baptism. In fact, this whole train of thought was stupid. She wasn't the problem. She needed a more open-minded family. But she couldn't come up with one of those in two weeks, which meant she was stuck. If she refused to obey like she did every other day of her life, she'd be breaking her promise to Wendy. Her sister would think she didn't care enough about her and Caleb to make the effort for one weekend of peace. And Jillian would do just about anything for the two of them. Even put up with the smell of cow shit—which may or may not be related to her brother-in-law Bob.

Fuck it. She was tired of thinking about it. She turned down "Thanks for the Memories" and opened one eye to see the dashboard clock. Time to face Thor ... who just so happened to be striding across the parking lot with a sack of equipment slung over his right shoulder.

The minute she pushed out of the car, he yelled, "Let's go, Bell! You wouldn't want to be late again."

The white rope from the netted bag was twisted around his wrist several times, and that made her think about tying him to her headboard again. *Fifty Shades of Jillian*, because this time, the woman would be in charge.

"Why not?" she asked facetiously.

He stopped and his gaze hardened. "Because the consequences would be heavy."

She bit back a laugh at how serious he looked. "What? Like paddling?"

His eyes widened for a brief second, and then he dropped the bag to the asphalt. "You have five minutes to get your ass on that field. Am I clear?"

"No paddling. Gotcha," she said, then she tossed him a grin. He probably didn't have the guts to paddle her even if he had the chance. *No game*, she thought, and she chuckled. What a shame.

When she made it to the field in full pads, Thor wasn't alone. Coach Howl and the defensive coordinator, Coach Linden, were gathered together near the goal post. But Thor saw her and made that stupid swirly motion with his finger. Laps. Again. How inspired.

"Dumb!" she yelled, but she jogged. "This is a waste of my time."

"Shut up and run, Bell!"

The suddenness and rudeness of it startled her, and she laughed. Aside from being a stern taskmaster, he seemed so proper—too proper for a rattled, middle-school comeback like "shut up." Hell, even his shirt was buttoned up tight and his pants lacked any discernible wrinkles. Too straight laced. Too perfect. Too *boring*. But hey, maybe Thor wasn't always as in control as he wanted people to believe. Maybe there was hope they could get along yet. But fifteen minutes later when she'd damn near run two miles, she hated his guts again.

"Bring it in, Bell!" He waved her over to join the rest of the team who had gathered on the red lightning bolt in the middle of the field with Coach Howl.

MJ and Tanya were smiling. "Do you resent the early arrival now?" Tanya asked.

Jade giggled.

Jillian drank from her water bottle with an extended middle finger in their direction then spread out far away from the three of them for stretches.

With one leg tucked behind her, she stretched out on the grass and stared at the blue sky. Things would get better. Once she got past this trip to Charity, things would go back to being focused on fun. She hummed "Bohemian Rhapsody" as she switched legs.

When they finally broke up into positional squads, she tried not to pay any attention to Thor. He was too long winded anyway. He wasted time explaining the "right way" to do things. There was no one right way, in Jillian's opinion. Whatever way amounted to points on the scoreboard worked.

"... and the way I see it, that's the problem," he rattled on. "There's a shocking lack of fundamentals here."

She rolled her eyes. *Yes, shocking.*

"How much film do you watch each week?"

Jillian yawned.

"Are we boring you, Bell?"

"Yes," she said without hesitation.

"You could always run some more."

Somebody snickered behind her.

"You could always get to the point," she countered.

Something lethal flashed in his eyes, and his mouth opened like he was going to blast her. His fists clenched, too, but then he shook them out slightly, and she had to admit the restraint was impressive and interesting. Usually guys who were wound that tight were begging to break loose.

He stared her down, now the picture of calm and reserve. How did he do *that*? If she had that skill, she could make it through forty-eight hours in Charity with no problem.

"The point is..." he leveled her with an icy glare that made his blue eyes brighter, "I'm instituting mandatory Sunday afternoon films until we're at .500."

Jillian didn't have to be a math teacher like Jade to know that even if they won the next two games, they wouldn't be at .500, which meant the Sunday of Caleb's baptism would be a "mandatory" film day. *Shit.* She was going to have to ask Thor for permission to go ... unless she circumvented him and asked his father. Coach Howl was the real man in charge, after all.

She grinned. Thor needed more than a hammer to keep her in line.

Chapter Three

Maybe the woman had a legitimate mental deficiency that made it impossible to keep her mouth shut. Carter watched Bell laugh and joke and hoot and holler and generally be a grade-A disruptive presence to practice ... unless she was actively engaged in a drill or had the ball. When she had the ball, it was—and he hated to admit it—intoxicating.

He watched her run routes with impressive precision. Her flexibility and adjustment instincts were top notch. Her hands were sure and soft. Her peripheral vision was sharp. And when she left the ground to snag a difficult ball out of the air, it was an art form.

He nodded with appreciation. But the minute the play was over, she shoved the defender and took off laughing, her lips flapping the whole way. His nod turned into a shake. That mouth was her biggest liability.

His father approached on the right. "How did they take the news?"

"Better than I expected." Most people raised serious hell when they were stripped of their only day off. But films weren't strenuous. They would survive. And hopefully, this would give them incentive to work harder and win.

"Excellent."

A rare smack of approval landed on Carter's back. *Nice.* He smiled.

"We'll let them process that for a few days before we completely eliminate Malloy's ineffective pass offense."

Another slap on the back, and his dad wandered away.

Carter's smile faltered. From what he could see, Malloy hadn't been entirely off the mark with his offensive plan. The quarterback was effective. He watched as MJ Rooney dropped back to pass. Carter noticed a hitch in her arm motion. Maybe he'd imagined it. As a former QB himself, he could be overly critical of the position. He squinted for a clearer view of her next pass. Yep, a hitch. He could fix that. And the receiving core? Jillian made a one-handed grab look easy. He whistled. Even better, she wasn't the only wide out here with natural talent. They were just sloppy. If he could instill some discipline in them, then he could make them productive.

But that wasn't what his father wanted. Dad worried that years of being known as *the* passing team in the league had finally caught up with them and made them too predictable. Defenses were honing in on Rooney and Bell and shutting them down with ease. According to his father, running the ball for a time would shock everyone. From what Carter could see, it shocked some of the Clash players, too, and he wasn't sure that was helping anybody.

After practice wound down and the players disappeared into the locker room, Carter helped secure the field equipment and then headed off to find his father. When he rounded the final stretch of bleachers, he saw Jillian storm out of the office and stomp into the locker room. Something had her fuming.

Carter grinned. Was it bad that he got satisfaction out of her frustration? Nah. She frustrated the hell out of him, so it was only fair. He still had no idea how he was going to get her to settle down like his father had requested.

Speaking of ... his dad appeared at the end of the hallway, shaking his head.

"What was that all about?" Carter asked.

"She wanted permission to miss a mandatory film day."

Of course she did. Carter smirked. "And she's mad that you said no."

"No, she's mad that I told her she needed to clear it with you."

Bell must've loved that. Still, he liked that his father was letting him have the say on this. Signs of respect were few and far between these days.

"Of course, you'll tell her no, but it's better she hears it from you. We need some serious player discipline. That's why I hired a Marine," his dad continued emotionlessly.

A Marine. Not "my son." Not even "a former NFL-caliber quarterback." He should've known. "I'll talk to her," he said flatly. No reason to prolong the ordeal.

"Take these," his father called out, halting him. "New running plays. I want to see some of these worked into your weekend game plan."

Carter took the pile of papers with a nod, then headed off to wait for her near the locker room door, telling himself that tackling the issue head on would save them time and aggravation—eventually.

"Good practice, Coach."

He nodded at a woman he didn't exactly recognize without her number on. "Yep, excellent work out there."

More women passed. They all greeted him with the same enthusiasm and respect. It felt good. He hadn't realized how much he'd missed being part of a football team. The positive feelings would only get better once this team was winning.

He glanced at his watch, wondering how long he should wait and if there was a chance she'd already made it out of here. *Nah, Bell will be last.* He wasn't a betting man, but he would put money on that. He'd only known her a couple days, but he could imagine her raising hell in the locker room just like she did on the field, especially after having words with his dad.

While he waited, Carter flipped through the pages his father had given him. He still thought he could make a pass offense work, but when someone in a position of authority asked you to do something, you did it. Period. Unless it was illegal. Throwing a few of these new plays into the weekend mix would mean even fewer pass plays. He could hear the loudmouthed protests from Bell now.

More women who weren't Bell walked by.

He looked at his watch again. He almost asked one of them if she was still in there. How the hell long did it take her to shower? In boot camp, he could do it in thirty seconds. Whole body. With an audience.

But then the locker room door opened, and out she came.

Her blue-tipped hair was now hanging loosely and looking a tad-bit wet. *Blue hair.* That was different.

"Ladies," he said, because she wasn't alone. A small group spilled out around her. The quarterback, Rooney, a linewoman whose name he couldn't recall, and the center, who wore number 60. Hey, he was learning.

He folded the wad of papers and stuffed them into his back pocket. "Bell, a word, please."

She hesitated and then glanced at her cohorts. "Catch ya later." Was that an eye roll?

Of course it was an eye roll.

He smiled at the rest of his offense. "See you tomorrow."

They smiled back. But not without some skittish glances in Bell's direction. Apparently even they knew she was one hell of a handful.

"Let's take a walk," he said.

A few steps in, she asked, "Why? Am I in trouble?"

"Should you be?" He could think of a few things she needed to be warned about. The disruption to otherwise orderly practices topped the list. But when he glanced at her, she looked confused.

In a flash, that confusion was gone, replaced by a lifted chin and hard stare. "Nope," she said. "I was here on time, I ran your laps, and I practiced hard."

True. "My father told me you went to him with a request, and he sent you to me. I wanted to save you the trip."

He stopped walking and faced her, wanting to see if his directness caught her off guard. Instead, he was struck by something else. She had freckles. Just a light dusting across the bridge of her nose, which was … unexpected. It softened her somehow.

But then mischief flashed in her copper-colored eyes, and he was on guard again.

"How chivalrous," she said, crossing her arms over her breasts. "And what did he tell you about my request?"

He glanced at her arm and the colorful mural that had been covered by long-sleeved Under Armor during the last two practices. One specific tattoo caught his eye. A 6-inch-tall Cinderella in a white, ripped ball gown, hair coming out of a bun, her face beautiful and serene as she wrung Prince Charming's neck. It was an impressive piece of artwork. Downright scary.

"That you want to miss a mandatory film meeting. Already," he said.

She dropped her arms to her sides, and for a minute, he thought she was going to walk away, but then she pulled her bottom lip between her teeth and batted her lashes. "So I guess this is the part where I beg."

What a piece of work. She was actually going to try playing him. But for some reason, knowing that didn't stop him from staring at her mouth a beat too long.

"So can I?"

He blinked and looked her dead in the eyes. "I can't answer that."

Her arms folded over her chest again, and her expression hardened. "Why not?"

"Because I don't know the details of why you want to miss, *and* you haven't proven yourself worthy."

She stepped closer. "What do I have to do to prove it?"

He ignored the strange heat their bodies were throwing off, and stepped back. "Well, for starters, you can show me some respect. Then you can tell me why you need to miss."

She looked pained. She hemmed and hawed. Finally, she said, "It's a family thing."

An unpleasant family thing. That or she hated the fact that he was forcing her to talk to him. "Listen ..." he ran a hand through his hair and tugged on the back of his neck.

"You have a tattoo!"

Before he could react, her hands were wrapped around his biceps, forcing his sleeve to his shoulder.

"Oh my God!" She cackled, and it vibrated through him. "Is that what I think it is?"

Her finger traced a spot on the underside of his upper arm, and he sucked in a quick breath to stop the shivers. "Marvin the Martian. Yes, it is," he said, and then he reached up with his other hand and pulled his sleeve back down.

Too bad the damage had already been done. His skin felt hot and tingly where her hands had been, and his mind felt fuzzy.

"How can you be such a douche and like the Looney Tunes?" She shook her head. "I love Wile E. Coyote and hate the Road Runner. Bet for you it's the other way around."

It was, but after the douche comment, he wasn't interested in playing her game.

She laughed again. And despite his annoyance with her, she looked more attractive.

"I don't know what shocks me more," she said. "That you actually messed up your body with a tattoo or that *that's* the tattoo you picked. Why Marvin?"

Well, hey. At least she was talking to him like a relatively normal human being now. Not trying to bait him and seduce him into giving her her way.

"Because he's cool," he answered reluctantly. Maybe this conversation would break the ice and be the start of her settling down.

She rolled her eyes, and he chose to simply smile. "Actually, the entire Michigan football team got tattoos one night, and I'd just come off a Looney Tunes bender, so…" he tapped his bicep, "there you have it." But not all of it. He wasn't about to tell her about the hours upon hours he'd curled up in the big king bed next to his sick mother, watching Looney Tunes and hanging on every weak smile.

"Do you only have one?"

He shook his head. "A few years after Marvin, I got this." He instinctively lifted his left pant leg to show off the semper fidelis tattoo on his calf.

Her eyes widened. "You're a Marine?"

"Yes, ma'am."

"Well, shit. That explains a lot doesn't it? My father was Army." She stared off into space with this goofy look on her face.

Again he noticed those freckles.

"Carter, when you're through…"

He glanced up to see his father standing on the other side of the bleachers waving him over. He nodded and then looked at Jillian. "So when is this family thing?"

"Not this weekend, but next."

Then it would be his bargaining chip. "You can go, as long as you aren't late, you practice hard, and you watch your mouth. I'll give you my final word later in the week."

Another eye roll. He fought the smile that time. "Deal?" he asked.

She seemed to think about it. "Fine." She held out a hand.

He grabbed it, and she squeezed hard. This woman did not back down.

It made him laugh. "Bell, you're a piece of work."

"That's what they all say." She sauntered away, hips swaying side to side, and the seductive motion brought to mind the conversation he'd had with Cris.

Carter liked asses, too. Admiring that particular ass was totally inappropriate, though.

He shook his head and thoughts of Jillian away, then he pivoted and strode over to his father.

Those freckles sure were cute.

• • •

Jillian lived in an apartment above the restaurant Tanya's mother owned. Mama Mary's was a South City staple, and it was packed this Thursday night, which was good, because that meant Jillian had been right to convince Mary to feature live music.

Despite the crowd and the lively music, all Jillian could think was ... "He's a Marine."

"Why do you keep saying that?" Tanya asked from across the bar. "It's not that surprising. He acts like a drill sergeant most of the time, especially around you."

She stuck her tongue out and angled her body so she could see her band, ChixDigIt, dive into another set. They opened with "99 Red Balloons"—her favorite—but that nagging thought kept echoing in her brain. Carter Howl had something major in common with her father, *and* he had the authority to make her behave. If she didn't, he could bench her. Talk about incentive.

"What if you screw up, and he doesn't give you permission to go after all? Will you go anyway?" Jade asked.

"Thanks for the vote of confidence," Jillian said, appalled. "I'm not going to screw up. I can be good—if I want to be. I just don't usually want to be." She grinned.

A rough-looking guy with a nose ring approached the bar. He was cute in that skinny, goth sort of way. After she'd dumped Keller and left home, she'd gravitated to nothing but the anti-Prince Charming. Now, she attracted them by the truckload. Maybe it was the line of work.

"So, Mary tells me you're the band's promoter." His voice was scratchy. "I'm Groll, own a bar down the street. I couldn't help but notice the numbers of people she's been bringing in on Thursdays. We should talk."

Groll. She smiled. "Of course we should." She handed him her business card. "Call me anytime."

"I was hoping we could talk now." He sort of pushed his way into the gap between her and Jade, smelling like cigarettes. "How much?"

He was rude, but she was used to it, and more importantly, he was a potential gig. She plastered on her eager-to-please, party-girl face and got down to business, shouting over the band, who'd kicked it up with another eighties classic.

"Book 'em Thursday through Saturday and it's four hundred bucks. Play or pay." She'd had enough last-minute cancellations to learn quickly that their fee needed to be a guarantee.

He looked at her lips and his thumb swiped a quick line across the back of her neck. "Any way I could convince you to cut that fee? I'm a new bar, man. Receipts are low. Especially when I'm competing with this."

She scanned his body, which was firm if slim, and several ways immediately popped into mind. That little devil on her shoulder whispered, *It could be fun.* But she didn't need more fun right now. She needed to focus on Charity.

"No," she said. "Fees are set."

They talked a bit more and agreed to meet again after he'd had time to think about it. Then he stood and walked out with her business card in hand.

"He likes you," Tanya said with a grin. "What if you took him home to Charity?"

They laughed. For any other occasion, Jillian would've loved the shock value, but not for Caleb's christening.

The music slowed, and Jillian caught herself staring into space again. Carter Howl was a Marine. He was clean cut, straight laced, exactly the kind of Prince Charming her parents would love. She frowned.

If she was going to take anyone, it should be him.

Chapter Four

"We're going to win this one," Carter said in the pregame huddle once his father had been heard.

He'd put together a solid game plan, one that utilized the run but didn't forsake their passing capabilities. He glanced at Bell, who was buzzing, jogging in place. She whooped every few seconds and smacked helmets so hard he started worrying the players on the receiving end would get concussions. But he had to admit, he loved her enthusiasm. He might not show his excitement like that, but he felt it in his gut.

"This is our field, our crowd, our game," he said. "Let's go out there and win."

The women cheered as the sideline huddle broke up. He watched the offense take the field, and a part of him wanted to run out there with them. No matter how long it had been, it was still a part of him.

His father's hand landed on his back. "Today's the day we turn this thing around." He looked so certain, holding a laminated card of running plays in his weathered hands.

But Carter wasn't so sure. After one week of run-heavy practice, the team still didn't look sharp, and the first few minutes of the game proved it. After a fumble on the very first possession, the Pittsburgh defense had them so clearly predicted that it was three and out two possessions in a row.

Carter scrambled to make adjustments, shelving a few of the running plays despite a look of disapproval from his father. The first pass play with Bell as the target yielded them 30 yards. That was all it took for them to find their rhythm.

But still, his father wasn't happy. "You'll get complacent, like Malloy," his father said as he walked past.

Carter wasn't a complacent kind of guy; he was a winning kind of guy. Was his father so hell-bent on ridding Malloy and his competing philosophies from the team that he was willing to forego the obvious path to success—a flexible mix of run and pass plays? If his father had ever been the kind of guy Carter could talk to, he would've said as much. Instead, he hoped to show him.

Four running plays later, Bell soared into the end zone. *See? It doesn't have to be all or nothing*, he wanted to say to his dad, but instead, he simply smiled and let the scoreboard speak for itself.

Jillian came over to the sidelines with the biggest smile on her face. "Hell yeah!" She must've bellowed it a dozen times.

He hid a laugh behind his clipboard and reminded the women that there were still three quarters to play. Most of those minutes were neck and neck, amid a volley of points scored. And at the start of the fourth, the Clash was up by only three.

"We need to run the ball more," his father said. "Stick to the plan."

The offense looked tired—except for Jillian, whose legs bounced while she sat on the bench during a defensive stand.

"I don't know..."

His father smacked the play card against the palm of his hand. "They'll be expecting the pass when we send the offense back out there. Crumpet's legs are still fresh."

"Fine. We'll run Crumpet until she fatigues. But then we're going back to Bell." Keeping that much energy sidelined was crazy.

"As OC, it's your call, but you shouldn't stray from the plan, and you shouldn't reward contrary behavior ... unless you want to look weak."

And that was his father's life philosophy in a nutshell, the reason Carter had been blacklisted for joining the Marines. He didn't want to be reminded of that now, so he nodded curtly and kept his distance for the next few possessions. He focused on the game—on winning the game.

When Crumpet fumbled on the 5-yard line, he felt somewhat vindicated, and that was no good. Letting his differences with his father amount to rooting against this team? No way.

He was relieved when Tanya Martin fell on the ball to recover the fumble.

Rooney called timeout on the field and met him on the sidelines. Out of the corner of his eye, he saw his father making a beeline toward them.

"Ring the Bell," he said quietly to Rooney, giving her the cue to get the ball to Jillian however she could, and then he gave her a pat on the ass and sent her back on the field.

His father's raised-brow look posed the question.

"We got this," was all Carter said. And then he settled in to watch.

The biggest difference between Carter's philosophy and his father's was that Carter believed a good QB had the best view of the field, which meant a good QB needed the room to call some shots. *Don't prove me wrong*, he thought.

In a blink, the O-line had let the pass rush make it up field, as Rooney flipped the ball to Bell, who cut up the middle. Five yards were all they needed for a touchdown, but Bell looked dead on the 1-yard line when a massive defender wrapped up her legs. Somehow, she high stepped out of the tackle and tumbled into the end zone. Carter glanced at the scoreboard and finally breathed. With a handful of seconds left, it was safe to say Bell had scored the winning touchdown, and on a shovel pass. Kind of the best of both worlds, considering the short pass resulted in a gutsy run. Would his dad notice that?

After the clock ran down, a few members of the team dogpiled on the 50-yard line.

Carter laughed at the enthusiasm. He couldn't blame them. Winning your first game after faithfully losing was pretty big. But then he glanced at his father. The man slapped a line coach on the back in what should've been a joyful, congratulatory gesture, only his eyes were trained disapprovingly on the field.

"Bring it in!" his father bellowed. Always conflicted. Never completely happy.

"Hell yeah!" Jillian hooted when she reached the sideline.

Carter soaked up her enthusiasm. He couldn't stop grinning. Whatever her discipline problems were, Bell was an undeniable star on the turf. She'd secured their first win of the season and made him look damn good in his coaching debut. In fact, he almost felt a little like he should reward her for that.

And he knew just the thing.

•••

"Party!" Jillian pulled a bottle of Jack from her duffle bag and shook it overhead. "Line up for a pour." The first win was something to celebrate.

"I can't," MJ said. "Tag and his family are waiting." She gave Jillian side-eye. "Why don't you wait until you get home? You drove, didn't you?"

Killjoy. Jillian stuck out her tongue at MJ's retreating back and turned to Tanya and Jade with a theatrical sigh. "Don't make me drink alone."

Tanya shook her head. "You know I can't."

Because her Super Bowl MVP boyfriend, Cam Simmons, had managed to make it into town.

Jillian wrinkled her face. "Whatever." She slung an arm around Jade's shoulders. "At least I have you."

"Yep, but later. I have to go for ice cream with Umma and Halmoni."

"Oh my God!" Jillian opened the bottle, took a swig, and weathered the burn. "Are you freaking kidding me?" She dragged the back of her hand over her mouth to catch an errant drop.

"Our first win of the season, and you'd rather get ice cream than drink with me?"

"They've been taking me for ice cream after my wins since my grandmother moved here. Like, back when I played micro soccer. It's still a big deal to them. You can come if you want."

God, that sounded painful. "I'll take a rain check. Just meet me at home when you're done, and then we'll go out." In the meantime, Jillian could pump up the music and pregame with a little Jack. She raised the bottle to her lips again, but Jade snatched it. "Oh, I see how you are. One for the road, huh?" Jillian teased.

But then Jade reached for the screw-on cap in Jillian's right hand.

"No." Jillian grabbed the bottle away from Jade with a generous splash to her Pink Floyd T-shirt.

"Bell!" Thor's voice ripped through the locker room, and for some reason, it scared the shit out of her. "If you're in there, I'd like a word."

"She's in here," a teammate yelled.

Gee, thanks. In a bit of dazed panic, she shoved the bottle at Jade and headed out to meet him.

"Hey!" he was smiling. He even closed the gap between them real friendly like, filling her face with his supremely manly scent. "What a great game! I wanted to tell you that..." His gaze dropped to the wet mark on her T-shirt, and then he made three exaggerated sniffs. "Do I smell alcohol?"

She swiped at the wet mark. "It's no big deal."

His jaw set. "I'll be the judge of whether or not it's a big deal. Were you drinking in there?"

She threw up her hands. "We just got our first win! I'm over twenty-one. It's not illegal."

"It's unnecessary! And it sets a bad example for your teammates."

"I don't see how."

"You wouldn't."

The words smacked of judgment. She hated being judged. "What's that supposed to mean?"

"No alcohol in the locker room, Bell. Do you hear me?"

She gave him a curt nod, and to her surprise, he turned and walked away. "Wait!"

He stopped and glanced over his shoulder, pure disgust in his eyes. "What?"

"Is that why you called me out here?"

"No." He tilted his head, and those blue eyes burned right through her. "I called you out to tell you you'd earned the right to skip films next Sunday." Happiness bubbled in her chest. "But I just changed my mind." He stalked off before she could have her say.

Oh yeah? Well ... She kicked the brink wall. Fuck him. She didn't need his approval. Like watching some shaky home movie of some other team was going to teach them how to win. That was bullshit! You learned by doing. You won by leaving it all on the field and never giving up. Not sitting in some smelly, dark locker room on a perfectly good day off. Big shock that Thor thought differently. He probably didn't make a move without consulting the rulebook he clearly had wedged up his ass. She was going to Charity, and she sure as hell didn't want him tagging along. She was crazy for ever thinking of it. Marine or not, she'd end up killing him before the weekend was through. No, she wouldn't want a damn thing from Carter Howl—even if he was the last man on earth.

She stormed back into the locker room and gathered up her things without saying goodbye to anyone, then cut through the back gates to the player parking lot. Freedom. Fun. That's what she needed.

She hopped into her car, turned the key, and the engine stuttered. Crap. That did not sound good. Neither did the sick, grinding wail. She tried again, and the engine whined for a split second but didn't turn over. One more time, and there was nothing but the telltale clicks. Her battery was dead.

Man, this was not her day! Good thing she knew her way around cars and she had cables. All she needed now was a host vehicle. She looked over the thinning lot. There was an empty car three spots away. Worst-case scenario, she could sit here and wait for the owner to return.

Out of the corner of her eye, she saw a flash of sapphire blue. A car—a really sweet car—was coming toward her. She hopped out of her stranded vehicle, raised her arms, and waved like hell.

• • •

Carter scrolled through satellite radio stations as he guided the car through the mostly empty lot. He had his eyes off the road for only a second, when he looked up and saw a body complete with a pair of arms waving in his path.

Jillian. After the confrontation outside the locker room, she was the absolute last person he wanted to see. Her T-shirt rode up her belly as she flagged him down, and it was hard not to appreciate the smooth curves of her waist and the subtle hips that weren't enough to keep her jeans from sliding down. His throat tightened. His skin heated. And his brain gave him less-than-chivalrous advice. *Drive right by. She's nothing but trouble.* But the honorable half of him wondered if she wasn't *in* some kind of trouble. He slowed his car to a stop.

Her face wrinkled the minute she saw it was him. "Never mind." She waved him off and looked around the parking lot.

"What's wrong?" he asked out his open window.

"Nothing. At least nothing that concerns you."

That let him off the hook. He could drive away and not feel guilty. Except, he would, especially if there was something he could've done. "Bell, quit being a hard ass and tell me what you need. If I can help, let me help."

She flashed a cocky look at him and then sauntered over to the car. The sudden change in her demeanor had him bracing for something.

Resting her forearms on the door, she leaned in the smallest bit. Her hair fell forward, carrying with it an unexpected floral scent. "Fine. If you want to play hero, then so be it." She reached in and traced her finger along the curve of his leather steering wheel, "I need a jump."

He sat a little straighter, and she shot him a dry but humored look, like she expected him to react this way. "I don't have jumper cables," he said. His throat was tight, but not nearly as tight as another part of him.

She pushed off his car, apparently having had her fun. "I do. I just need the juice." Her gaze ran the length of his car. "This bad boy looks like it has lots of juice. Dang." She drew out the word. "How can *you* afford this? Women's football pays squat, and the Marines can't be much better." But then she didn't seem to care about the answer, because she threw him a challenge with her wide eyes. "So, what's it gonna be? Are you gonna help me or not?"

He hesitated. She'd be better off calling a tow truck. He wasn't even sure a car like his should be used as a battery boost for—he glanced at the rust bucket she was driving—a car like that.

"Second thoughts, huh? Figures." She rolled her eyes. "Run along. I'll find somebody with a pair who isn't afraid to use them."

He knew she wasn't talking about a pair of jumper cables. The dig at his manhood irked him. "Move," he said gruffly. "So I can pull around. Or would you rather I come at you from behind?"

He grinned when a smidgeon of shock registered on her face.

Off in the distance, he saw his father's car pulling away. *Nothing to see here*, he thought. Just a man helping out a woman in need. But as he maneuvered the car, he snuck another peek at Bell, who was leaning over the hood of her car like an oil-and-lube calendar pinup. His skin hummed. God, he hoped he didn't live to regret this. He was already breaking out into a cold sweat.

She was waiting for him with cables in hand when he put his car in park and exited the vehicle.

A look of raised-brow superiority flashed across her face. "You need to kill your engine."

"Right." He reached in and hit the ignition button.

Her sarcastic smile said it all. "You've never done this before have you?"

Hell no. "Of course not. My car is reliable, and if it weren't, I would call roadside assistance."

She hummed knowingly. "Like my Dad always said, 'Living in luxury makes a man weak.'" She had the balls to wink. "Now, pop the hood."

Once he did as he was told, she leaned over his front end with the clamps in her hands, mumbling to herself the names of car parts—some he'd never heard. Then she asked him to open the trunk, saying something about European cars with "junk in the back."

He tried hard not to look at her ass.

The longer it took, the more he fidgeted against the sweat trickling down his spine. "Are you sure you know what you're doing?" This was a hundred-thousand-dollar car. He glanced at her beat up Volvo, again. When he looked back at her, she gave him a dirty look. "What?" he asked. "It's a reasonable question."

"I know what I'm doing," she said defiantly. "Worst-case scenario? It sparks. And sparks won't kill you." She tossed him a challenging look over her shoulder, and damn it if his temperature didn't climb a little higher. "Now, an explosion is another story. That would destroy your car and maim us."

Ugh. How the hell had he gotten himself into something this volatile? He was just about to put an end to the insanity, when she folded her arms atop her head and frowned.

"It's not going to work. Shit. Shit. Shit." She dropped her arms in a huff and walked a tight circle.

"I don't suppose you have any sort of roadside assistance coverage for that, do you?" he asked.

She wrinkled her face. "No." Again her arms landed atop her head, and she exhaled loudly. "I don't suppose you'd be willing to drive me to the auto parts store so I could pick up a new battery."

He was staring at her navel again. He didn't try to hide it, and he didn't bother questioning whether or not she could actually change a battery. He'd seen enough to assume she could. And a new battery would save *his* battery ... and possibly a whole lot more.

"Where's the nearest auto parts store?" He dragged his gaze from her midriff, pausing for a second on her perky breasts before he concentrated on her face.

She dropped her arms on a laugh. "Dude, you're like the worst man ever. It's a couple miles away. I can show you."

He weighed his options. If he stayed, Jillian might take another stab at juicing the battery—and that could kill his car. If he went, being stuck in close quarters with her might kill him.

Carter shrugged. Out of the frying pan and into the fire, like his mother had always said.

• • •

Jillian folded herself into the pristine BMW, her heart leaping out of her chest. Exactly *how successful* was Carter Howl? Surely every Marine couldn't afford a car with an engine so sophisticated she couldn't even pull off a simple battery jump. What the hell did this guy *really* do? Before that crack about coming at her from behind, she would've expected something boring, an accountant or worse. But now, she didn't have a clue.

She rattled off the basic directions to the auto parts store, and then opened his glove box on a whim. Maybe something in here would tip her off to his occupation. She got sidetracked with the cleanliness—so organized it was creepy. He was completely opposite from her. Which was no surprise after he'd basically criminalized her measly celebratory drink. She rolled her eyes as she rummaged through a stack of loose papers. He even had a plastic expandable folder labeled "maintenance."

"Looking for something?" His voice was loud and rough enough to unnerve her.

She shut the box and wished she'd sat on her hands the minute she'd gotten into the car. That was a trick her mother had taught her to do when little Jillian was overly excited and impulsive. Which was damn near all the time.

But her curiosity about him wasn't satisfied. "What do you do for a living? Are you still a Marine?"

"Once a Marine, always a Marine." He grinned.

It made her woozy. Or maybe that was the overwhelming scent of man and top-grade leather seats. She needed to crack a window.

"I'm no longer active duty, though." He drove with two hands on the wheel and pretty damn close to the old ten-and-two position she'd learned in driver's ed. *Rule follower.*

"Have you ever been to a Shock & Awe?" he asked.

She made a face. "That sell-out, pseudo-gamer bar? Unfortunately. I can't believe they made it a chain. I wouldn't go back if you paid me."

He grimaced. "Well, they do pay me. In fact, I'm the founder and CEO."

Niiice. Little Jillian used to get her mouth taped shut, too, rarely and only in extreme situations. Some duct tape would've been handy about five minutes ago. Nothing like poking the bear.

"Sorry," she said. "Not that you're the CEO, but that I insulted your company."

"Eh." He brushed her insult off. "No worries. You're actually not the first person to say something negative. Last week, customer service forwarded an e-mail from a woman who called the place a 'hell hole that contributed to the moral decline of our youth.'"

Jillian laughed. "Well, I'm not exactly worried about the moral decline of anyone. In fact, I would've written back and thanked her for the compliment. But what'd you say?"

"Nothing. I learned a long time ago when you're dealing with extremists that it's best not to engage them unless you're prepared for one hell of a fight."

"You learned that in the military," she said knowingly. Her father had made similar comments.

Carter nodded. His profile was striking and strong, but there was an unexpected softness, too. She had the urge to slip her hand over his cheek and run her fingers through his hair just to know what it felt like. He was definitely somebody's Prince Charming. She stole a peek at his empty ring finger. *Hm.*

"It's Saturday night, she said. "Don't you have someplace to be? Somebody to see?"

He glanced at her. "Are you poking into my personal life, Bell?"

She shrugged. "Just curious."

"I'm currently single," he said.

But that didn't mean he didn't have somebody waiting on him tonight. He was handsome, upstanding, successful, and a Marine to boot. A lot of girls were interested in that sort of thing. Yeah, her parents would probably die if she showed up with someone like this. She laughed.

The car stopped at a red light and he looked at her. "What's so funny about that?"

"I don't know. It's just funny."

He frowned. Hell, he even looked good doing that. "If you say so," he said, his eyes roaming her face. His gaze seemed to linger on her lips, and his frown relaxed.

Suddenly it didn't feel very funny anymore.

"So you're an Army brat?" he asked.

She nodded. "But that's a bunch of crap. My sister moved around as much as I did, and she's an angel. That nickname gives all Army kids a bad rep, when only a handful of us deserve it."

His brow dipped. "You don't seem so bad. You just need a little focus."

That's what the pediatrician had said when she was put on Ritalin at ten. It had kept her up all night and made it hard to eat. She would take the bad rep over the drug-induced focus any day, but he was being nice, wasn't he? "Thanks, I think," she said wryly.

A weird silence settled over the car as they stared at each other until his face washed in a green glow. "The light's green."

In a flash, he was looking out the windshield again and pulling through the intersection way too fast. She gripped the edge of the seat with both hands. *Ha!* The methodical Marine had a lead foot. But almost immediately, he backed off. A few seconds later, she noticed people passing them, and when they couldn't, they rode his ass like a saddle. A minute passed. Then two.

She laughed. "You have to go faster."

"No, I don't. I'm going the speed limit."

"Nobody but old people drives the speed limit. Then again, how old are you?"

He tossed her a wounded look. "How old do you think I am?"

That smile. Every time he unleashed it, it took her by surprise and curled her toes. "Thirty-two?"

He feigned horror. "You're benched, Bell." But then he smiled again. "Just kidding. I turned thirty in November."

"Well, that's still way too young to be driving like you're eighty. Pick it up to at least your age."

To her surprise, he did.

A funny feeling came over her, carrying with it a crazy thought. Maybe Carter Howl wasn't the asshole she thought he was. Maybe she could just talk to him ... normally.

She cleared her throat. "Uh, about earlier." She squeezed her hands together in her lap, "You know, the booze? If it's off limits in the locker room, then I won't bring it again. Promise."

"It's off limits."

"Okay. Done deal. From now on, the locker room is dry—just like my hometown." She laughed nervously.

He parked the car in a spot near the auto shop's front door, and then he faced her. "Where's your hometown?"

"Charity, Pennsylvania," she said. "I was born there but left before I started school, and then my parents moved back there after my father retired. It's a barrel of laughs."

He nodded. "Is that where you're supposed to be going next weekend?"

Her stomach flipped at the thought. "Yep. Unless, you tell me I can't." Which suddenly sounded like a reasonable alternative. She could blame her absence on her big, bad football coach. Then she could see Wendy and Caleb another time. But Caleb's looming surgery coupled with the rest of the football season wouldn't make rescheduling easy. She sighed and reached for the door handle.

"You can go," he said. "I won't pry about the details, but it seems important. *Family* is important. Just don't make me regret it, Bell."

She nodded and pushed out of the car. Maybe she should've thanked him. She just wasn't sure he'd done her any favors.

He didn't follow her into the store, and she welcomed the break from him. She wandered the aisles aimlessly, knowing full well the battery she needed would be behind the counter. No rush.

Her phone buzzed. Jade texted that she was on her way home from having ice cream. And still, there was no sense of urgency.

Maybe Jillian would get the battery and tell Carter to go home. She could walk back to the stadium. She didn't need him anymore.

But when she opened his car door and he smiled at her, she sat instead. When she wasn't so aggravated with him that she wanted to scratch his eyeballs out, there was actually something very calming about him. Like he'd be a good guy to have on your side in a fight. Maybe that was just the whole Thor thing talking.

"All set?" he asked.

"All set." She stretched her arms over the battery box and strummed a simple beat with her thumbs.

Out of the blue, he asked, "What do you have against Prince Charming?"

She glanced up and saw him staring at her tattoo. "Um, well, he's fake—too good to be true."

"But did she have to kill him?" He chuckled. "Seems extreme."

"Nah. It's symbolic. She was just looking to get away from him permanently. What's more permanent than death?" Jillian looked at him and smiled, but he didn't smile back.

In fact, for a few seconds, he looked downright concerned, but then he shook whatever was bothering him off and asked, "Are you Cinderella?"

She twisted her arm and eyed up the tattoo again. How much did she really want to tell him? Normally, she didn't like people who pried. Sometimes, she even lied just to end the discussion. But again, she felt this weird pull to him, like she would be safe— if she wanted to be.

"I was engaged at nineteen."

"Wow. That's young," he said.

She shrugged. "Typical though in Charity. Half my high school class was engaged by graduation. We had a future homemakers club with more members than the football team."

"Damn," he said. "I take it it's a small town."

"Yep. No stoplights, four churches."

He nodded. "Doesn't seem to fit you."

"Hell no. But everybody else in my family loves it. Even my younger sister stayed. She drank the Kool-Aid and wound up married with a baby." Jillian grinned cynically. "I only narrowly escaped."

He seemed to suddenly realize they were still sitting in the parking lot, and he put the car in reverse and guided it from the spot. She figured he'd heard enough, but then he asked, "How often do you go back?"

She itched to turn on the radio and end the conversation, but she heard herself say, "Rarely, thank God. Last time was two years ago for my sister's wedding."

He kept his eyes on the road. "And this time? If you want to tell me."

She fidgeted. "My sister, Wendy, is having Caleb's christening next weekend."

"And you're dreading it?" he finished, but it didn't sound like a question.

"Yeah." Carter went silent. "For a lot of reasons," she continued. Still no sound from the driver's seat. She could probably stop now, end it there, but the rest of the story felt heavy in her mouth. "You could say I don't have many supporters in town, my brother-in-law included." She looked at Carter, who stared straight ahead. Why wasn't he saying anything? Why was she saying everything? *Shut up*, she thought. But then he nodded slowly, and that was all the encouragement she needed. "My ex-fiancé who inspired this tattoo will be there." She held up her arm. Carter glanced at it and raised his eyebrows, but still, he didn't speak. "The whole town looks at me like I'm some kind of zoo animal, and I'm just so sick of it. Usually I'd tell them to shit in their hats and pull it over their ears. Believe me. I've done it plenty of times before. But this time, Wendy has made me swear to be on my best behavior." She exhaled loudly. "I'm not sure I can be, and she's the one person I don't want to disappoint. Again." Was that a smirk on his face?

"Listen…" he turned onto the four-lane road that led to the stadium. "Sometimes no matter how good your intentions, you'll still end up disappointing someone. And it sucks. I know 'cause I've been there."

She blinked. Thor understood? *That* man with *this* car had been a disappointment to somebody? No way.

"I don't suppose you're free next weekend," she said with a laugh. "You could go with me and keep in me in line."

The car took a dramatic dive in speed. "Like a chaperone?" he asked.

"No. God, no. I'm kidding." But she wasn't. Not really. And that was the biggest joke of all. "Forget I said it. All of it. I was just … babbling."

She snuck a look at him. He was staring straight ahead, gripping the steering wheel at ten and two, looking awfully intense. What a weird night this had turned out to be.

"I have mandatory films on Sunday," he said. "Besides, I'm not sure what my dad would say. It's kind of…"

Crazy.

"… improper."

"No shit it's improper. It involves me." She grinned. "But seriously, don't worry about it." She slapped her hands on the battery box for emphasis. "Forget it."

The quiet that followed drove her crazy. She chewed on a hangnail. She bounced one leg. She contemplated jumping out at the next red light.

"Is this more about being there for your nephew or getting back at your ex?" he finally asked.

"My nephew. Absolutely. The ex just complicates things because everyone in town thinks he's the saint—well, because he's the town preacher"—Carter flashed her a look—"and I am, of course, very clearly the sinner." *Which on a Saturday night was not at all bad*, she told herself. She would get this battery hooked up and be dancing by 10:00.

Carter shook his head again and again, but he remained silent as they pulled into the stadium. Not often, but sometimes, she wished she could keep her mouth shut.

"Let me think about it," he said.

The words tripped her up as she was climbing out of his car. "Um, okay," she said slowly. "Thanks for the help tonight."

She scrambled off to her car before any other "improper" requests slipped out.

Had she really just asked him to go to Charity? Ha! Talk about impulsive. Of course, odds were he wasn't seriously considering it. But what if he did come? Oh my God! The look on people's faces. The look on Keller's face! Let him look her in the eye and tell her again how she would never find a man better than him. She glanced back at the gleaming luxury car and its chiseled-to-perfection driver. Oh yeah, this could be good—real good.

Chapter Five

Walking into his sister Amanda's perfectly decorated colonial on a Sunday evening felt a lot like walking into his parents' house when his mother had been alive. Same froufrou taste in decorating. Same yummy scents wafting down the hall from the kitchen. Same family portrait the Howls had sat for back when he was ten.

"How do you work this new remote? It's time for tip-off."

Same sports-obsessed guy barking commands from Amanda's living room couch.

Carter chuckled and then said a silent prayer of thanks, because there were years shortly after he'd enlisted when he wasn't welcomed around his father—the man's disappointment in his son had been that thick.

Who would've thought that Carter had something in common with Jillian Bell outside a love of football? And now he couldn't forget it—or the way she'd opened up last night and looked surprisingly vulnerable. That's why he'd said he'd think about it.

He had no business getting involved in a player's personal life, but he was the kind of guy who helped. And he had a hunch that smoothing the rift between her and her family would go a long way toward settling her down, which would benefit the team. Of course, hunches could be dead wrong.

He shrugged out of his jacket and hung it on the rack by the door.

"We got a Smart TV," Amanda's husband Nick said as he passed through the entrance hall on his way to the living room where Carter's father was still complaining. "It works with an iPad app." Nick turned his head and called into the living room, "Be right there, Dad." Then he patted Carter on the back. "Amanda is in the kitchen."

Like his mother, his sister showed love through her cooking.

"Hey." Carter came up behind her as she was standing at the sink and planted a kiss on her temple. The oven timer beeped.

"Hey, you," she said with a distracted smile. "Grab that. Potholders are on the island."

He glanced at his sister-in-law at the kitchen table, who was spooning something Army green into his nephew's mouth. "How's it going, Ruthie?"

"It's going in, but it's coming right back out," she said with a laugh.

After he took care of the pan, he made his way over to the highchair and kissed Rowen on the head. It was the only clean place on him. "You're making a mess, little man. Just like your daddy."

"What about his daddy?" Russ walked in from the other room with a squirming Katherine on his hip.

"You want to go to Uncle Carter," Russ said. "He can chase you around for a little bit."

The second oven beeped.

"Uncle Carter is busy helping Aunt Amanda. Chop-chop, kitchen boy," Ruthie said.

"Let's trade," Russ said.

"Nope. Ovens I can handle." He snatched the mitts off the counter. "Dogs I can handle. Terrorists I can handle. Toddlers scare the crap out of me."

He opened the oven and hoisted a covered metal pan from the middle rack.

"Because you scare the crap out of them," Russ said.

"Literally," Amanda added with a laugh.

Carter dropped the mitts. "I don't know why they all shit when I'm holding them."

"Language," his sister-in-law said.

"Too late. I heard it." The words were followed by a giggle that lit a spark in his heart and carved a smile on his face.

"Hey, peanut," he turned and said to his oldest niece, Sophia, who bounded down the back staircase. As usual, one hand was glued to her cellphone.

When she reached him, she threw her arms around his waist, and he squeezed until she squealed.

Almost eleven years ago, this child roared into his self-obsessed life and rocked his world. The minute he'd laid eyes on her in his sister's arms, he'd wanted to give her everything. He'd wanted to make that world a better place. He'd wanted her safe and happy. And he'd wanted his mother there to share in the joy. Since he'd been powerless over that last wish, a week after Sophia's birth, he'd found a way to have some control over the others ... he'd enlisted. And man, did that kick off a chain of unfortunate events.

His father had accused him of being careless and acting on a whim, even though military service had been pulling at Carter since he'd been sixteen and trying to make sense of his mother's cancer. For a while, there'd been tension between him and his brother, Russ, who'd said enlistment was nothing but an escape from the pressure at home. Only Amanda seemed to get him. She called it a personal crusade for purpose and meaning wrapped up in an extreme desire to do something profound in honor of Sophia's birth. If he'd been good with words, that's exactly what he would've said.

"Wednesday's picture of Herky got three hundred likes!" Sophia was practically jumping out of her skin.

"Wednesday? Wednesday?" He was trying to think of what made Wednesday so special.

"He was in your bed!"

Riiight. The sneak. Carter had kicked him out immediately after taking the picture.

"The dog was in your bed? OMG." Russ did his best impression of a preteen girl and feigned horror. "Did you burn your sheets?"

"No," Carter said dryly. "I washed them."

"With bleach. Twice." Of course, Amanda had to get in on the fun.

"Did he get yelled at?" Sophia asked. Those puppy dog eyes told him exactly where this was going.

"He was reprimanded."

Her eyebrows crowded together at the top of her pug nose. "Did you use your Marine voice?"

"Yes."

She huffed. "Then he got *yelled* at, and I'm not happy about it."

Russ chuckled. "Me either, Soph. Uncle Carter is sooo mean."

Carter shot him what could be called his Marine look, which was tantamount to a "Fuck You."

"He deserves a warm bed, too," Sophia said.

"He has a nice dog bed in a warm house. I'd say that's pretty darn good for an animal."

"Then why does he want to be in your bed?"

Russ about busted a gut.

Carter pitched a potholder at him.

"Boys!" Ruthie yelled. "Behave."

Sophia and Amanda were laughing, too.

"I'll tell you what," Carter said. "If you want him in a real bed so badly, I'll bring him over here and he can sleep with one of you."

"Don't you dare!" Amanda smacked him between the shoulder blades with a roll of plastic wrap. "No pets."

Just like Mom. He loved that the older his sister got, the more similarities appeared. It didn't seem like such a loss when he could look at Amanda and see parts of his mother still here.

"What's all the racket in there?" his father called in from the other room. It might've bothered Carter that the man was still glued to the television if it wasn't for the laughter in his voice.

His family was a handful, but he loved every minute of it. Again, he thought about the lonely years when it seemed like his father and Russ didn't want him around. Being home on leave had been so stressful he'd eventually stopped coming to Cleveland—until Amanda e-mailed him pictures of then toddler Sophia and begged him to be an active part of her life. Something else he had in common with Jillian: pushy sisters.

Amanda passed him a stack of plates, and he headed for the dining room. A grainy image of a rattled Jillian lingered in his head. She was so worked up about going home that she'd asked him to help her survive the weekend. That was bat-shit crazy. They didn't see anywhere near eye to eye. But still, he was thinking about it and wondering if he shouldn't talk it over with his dad.

For the umpteenth time since he'd dropped Jillian off and watched her deftly change the battery, he shoved thoughts of her from his head. He helped his sister and brother-in-law set the table while Russ and Ruthie put their little ones down for naps. Then Dad came in like clockwork when the pot roast was served.

"Join hands, and we'll say grace," his father said.

Carter grabbed onto Amanda and Sophia.

"Lord, bless this food and those that have humbly prepared it in your name. Know that we thank you from the bottom of our hearts for the nourishment and companionship around this table. Extra special thanks for the Clash win yesterday." He opened one eye and flashed a quick smile at Carter. "In Jesus's name, Amen."

Amens circled the table, and then everyone dug in. Plates clattered. Voices chattered. Carter sat back and took it all in. This was what life was all about—why he'd put his life on the line in service to his country. *Everyone* deserved a chance at peace and love like this. *Jillian, too.* He shook off the thought and passed a bowl of green beans to Sophia.

She wrinkled her nose and then smiled prettily. "No, thank you."

"Vegetables are good for you, Soph." He pushed the bowl toward her again.

She eyed up his plate. "Then why don't you have any?"

Busted. "Shh." He grinned and set the bowl in the middle of the table.

After dinner, most of them cleared the table, loaded the dishwasher, and cleaned the kitchen, while Dad and Nick returned to the TV. Russ refilled wine glasses and opened fresh beers.

"So what's your take on women's football?" Russ asked.

"It's football," Carter said emphatically. "That's my take."

"I don't like football," Sophia said.

Carter snagged her around the shoulders and rubbed his knuckles on her head. "Peanut, I think you were adopted. What kind of Howl doesn't like football?"

"I'm a Williams," she said.

"Ooh, burned!" Russ laughed.

"Half Williams, half Howl," Amanda corrected. "All attitude," she added under her breath.

But Carter kind of liked the attitude. It had spark.

Against his will, he thought of Jillian. Again.

"I don't like football either, Soph," Ruthie said. "Most women don't."

Carter scoffed. "Dad and I coach an entire team of women who love football."

"I just can't see taking that seriously," Russ said. "The one and only game I saw looked like a bad high school game. Boring as hell."

"You saw an off game, then," Carter said.

"What are they like?" Ruthie asked.

"Um, they're normal women who like football. I'm not sure what you mean by that." But he did, and it rubbed him the wrong way.

"I don't know. I picture them being really manly."

He scoffed. "Not at all."

"So there are attractive women football players." Russ bobbed his eyebrows.

Carter scowled. "Stick a dishrag in it, Weasel."

"Ooh!" Amanda tapped her wedding ring on the side of her wine glass. "That means he thinks somebody is cute. Dish."

"No, and lower your voice." Their father was in the other room. The last thing he needed was his dad thinking he was prowling around the hen house.

"I think you're right, Amanda," Ruthie said. "Otherwise he wouldn't care if Dad heard."

They were relentless. "Fine. Some of them are very attractive." He rationalized this by thinking the women would probably be happy to hear this. It was a compliment after all. "The QB, a few linewomen." He scratched alongside of his eye. "A wide receiver … or two."

"Sounds like fertile mating grounds," Russ said.

"Pig!" Ruthie backhanded him in the belly.

Russ buckled over. "What I meant to say was fertile *meeting* grounds. You could stand to meet somebody who sticks around long enough to meet the family."

Skeptical sounds filled the kitchen.

"He won't meet somebody like that until he relaxes his expectations a little bit," Amanda said.

She sounded like Cris, who was still advising him to "pick a woman and do something crazy."

The craziest thing he could think of involved Jillian Bell and a little town called Charity.

• • •

When Jillian walked into the kitchen Sunday night after a good, long nap, Jade sat at the table hidden behind her laptop screen.

"Hey, Sleeping Beauty," Jade said.

Jillian squinted in the fluorescent lights and yawned. "Hey."

Jade chuckled. "What's on your agenda for the evening?"

"No clue." She'd hoped a long nap after films would've rid her mind of Carter, but no such luck. The first thing she thought when she opened her eyes had been, "Was he really thinking about it?"

He hadn't said a word about Charity that morning at films—not that she'd expected him to say anything in front of the team and his father. But she'd been a little surprised he didn't call her aside when films were over—to say he must've been delusional to consider it. A work-related call had stolen him from the room, and she never saw him again. Now she was stuck in this weird limbo. Seriously. If this worked out, he could be the ace in her pocket.

She crossed the kitchen in search of Advil for the headache that wouldn't quit. That's when she noticed the most annoying voice in the world coming from Jade's laptop.

"James is about as genuine as the slimeball who sold me my first used car, the one that had me looking up Ohio lemon laws a week later. Loooozzzer. And the Cavs are the bigger losers as long as they're buying what he's selling."

Jillian grabbed her head, covering her ears and muffling the sound. "What the hell are you listening to?"

"Sports talk radio. I stumbled on this guy while I was trying to find coverage of the Dayton game. He's a jerk, isn't he?" She rolled her eyes. "The show's called, 'Riled Up with Rome' and you should hear the people who call in and argue with him. They're all crazy."

"Get out of the gene pool!" Rome yelled at a caller.

Jillian waved a hand dismissively. "Shut him off. I already can't think straight."

Jade hit a button on the keyboard, silencing the talk show. "Why? What are you thinking so hard about?"

"Stuff."

"Family stuff?"

Jillian didn't answer. She popped the pills into her mouth and swallowed them dry. Then she strolled over to the sound system, hooked up her MP3 player, and sighed happily as a soothing guitar riff filled the room. Much better than Jade's questions and bigmouthed Rome.

She made her way back into the kitchen and grabbed an apple from the basket.

"So, you're not going to answer me?" Jade talked while she typed.

Jillian plopped down in the chair across from her. "I was thinking about family stuff, but I don't want to talk about it."

Jade nodded. "Fair enough. But you know, talking might help."

She bit into the apple and chewed. Talking seemed to help last night, except when she said too much and ended up asking Carter to Charity. She was going to call and let him off the hook. He didn't really want to do it anyway. He was just being nice and ... She remembered the moment when they'd connected over something from his past—something that had been a disappointment to someone else. What had he done that had been so bad?

"Gimme your laptop." she said.

"No. I have ten more algebra questions to come up with for tomorrow's homework. Then you can have it."

She didn't suppose she could argue with that, so she focused on the music and polished off the apple. When she reached the core, she asked, "Are you done yet?"

Jade hit a button emphatically. "No, what's your big hurry anyway?"

"I want to Google search Carter to see if he's hiding anything, something big—like prison time."

Jade looked up. "Why would you think that? Wasn't he in the Marines? I don't think you can be in the military if you have a criminal record."

Good point. "Well, maybe it's not criminal. He said something last night when he was helping me with the battery, and it made me think maybe he's been in trouble. Now I'm curious."

"You're calling him Carter now? What happened to Thor?"

Jillian shrugged. "That's his name." It wasn't a big deal, but Jade's brows lifted like it was. Whatever. "You take too long," Jillian said, and she stood up to throw out the apple core. "I'm going to shower."

She shuffled to her room, gathered up her robe, and grabbed some towels. Despite the weirdness of the last twenty-four hours, there was one positive. Carter had given her permission to miss films on Sunday, which meant she could finally meet her nephew. She lifted her phone off the alarm-clock charger and opened Wendy's last text, which contained a picture of Caleb. He looked so small wrapped in a yellow blanket and sleeping in her father's burly arms. She smiled at the sweet face and swiped her fingers over the screen to zoom in.

Going home wouldn't be easy, but it was the right thing to do.

The phone vibrated. Incoming call. She didn't recognize the number, so she declined it. If someone was calling to book a band, she would call them back before she showered.

New Voicemail Message

Popped up on the screen, and she plopped down on her bed to listen. She nearly dropped the phone when she heard a smooth, deep voice say, "Bell, it's Carter Howl. I've been considering everything you said last night, and well, believe it or not, I want to help."

Oh. My. God. She threw herself back on the bed and replayed his message.

What had she gotten herself into now?

Chapter Six

Carter watched Jillian pour way too much sugar into her third cup of coffee and glanced at his watch.

7:45 p.m.

On a Sunday evening. "How are you going to sleep after all that caffeine?"

"I don't sleep much," she said. "It's been that way my whole life. I'm a night owl. That's probably something you should remember this weekend."

He looked at the reverse side of the neon open sign hanging in the window of the diner around the corner from his condo. He'd invited her here to discuss how he could help her get through her nephew's christening, but it was clear, she already had a few ideas of her own.

"My boyfriend would know if I'm up all night and sleep all day." She grinned.

He was not her boyfriend. He was some schmuck who had gotten himself in too deep. "I don't want to lie to them."

She rolled her eyes as she sipped from a white mug. "Right. So we stroll into town as what? Friends?"

"Sure." He put his hand over his water glass when the waitress offered more and mouthed a "No, thank you."

"Men and women aren't close friends in Charity," Jillian said. "You're either related or you're married or you respectfully interact. But you don't bring home a guy and introduce him to the family unless you're dating. If you're doing this, you're doing this as my boyfriend."

He sighed. Being in a subordinate position was not for him, but she knew her family and the town better than he did. "Fine. Then we're dating." His mouth curled around the word. He didn't like it one bit, but he wanted this mission to be a success. "What else do I need to know?"

"My mother's name is Karen. She goes to church three times a week, cooks with twice the butter any recipe needs, and hangs clothes out on the line even in winter. Her pet peeves are women who color their hair, tattoos, and people who don't take their shoes off inside her house. As you can see, I'm two out of three." Somehow Jillian managed a convincing eye roll and a smile at the very same time.

"I have tattoos," he said. "And I wear shoes in my house. Looks like I'm two out of three, too. You'll be in good company."

"Not in Charity. We'll keep our tats covered, which means long sleeves for me and no shorts for you." She seemed to consider that as her eyes scanned him from the top of his head to the point where his waist dropped behind the table. With a *tsk-tsk* she said, "That sucks. I bet you have nice legs." She slapped a hand on the table. "Wait. What do you sleep in? Pajama bottoms or boxers?" Her smile grew until it glowed. "You sleep naked, don't you?"

He choked out a laugh. "No." Heat climbed up his face, and he told himself not to let her get to him. Concocting a cover story, deceiving a family—even if his intentions were admirable—was serious business. "What I sleep in is irrelevant. I'll be dressed in church clothes while we're there."

"Oh." Her mouth shut, and she stared at him blankly. "I told Wendy we were spending two nights. She's so excited."

Warning bells sounded in his head. A weekend sleepover? No way in hell. "I work Monday."

She didn't look impressed. She took another drink of her coffee and said, "You own the company. I'm sure nobody argues with you when *you* come in late or want a day off." She let that jab sink in before continuing. "I want to spend the night on Saturday so I'm not late for the Sunday service."

God knew she needed help with the whole timing thing. But spending *two* nights? Spending those nights with her? Not that they were going to be sleeping in the same bed. He felt pure heat at the base of his neck. Did she think they would be sleeping in the same bed? "How would that even work?"

"What do you mean?"

"I mean ... if we spend the weekend ... together..." as he stammered, she sat up straighter, and her eyes shined brighter, "where would we sleep?"

She was loving every minute of this. "Well..." She propped an elbow on the table and tapped two fingers against her full lips. "My childhood bed is a little small, but it's very comfortable. We'll just have to cuddle." He was about to motion for the check and tell her he wasn't willing to go that far, when she let him down with the hitch of one perfectly arched brow. "Do you think my mother would ever allow that? She'll make us sleep on opposite ends of the house. She doesn't approve of 'shacking up' or anything that insinuates premarital sex." She shrugged. "Maybe you'll end up on the pull-out in the family room, unless they got a new mattress for the daybed in her sewing room. God was that a nightmare." He opened his mouth to ask why, but Jillian waved a dismissive hand. "I ruined the old one."

He wasn't about to ask how she'd ruined the mattress. Instead, he cleared his throat and said, "Well, *if* I agree to spend the night, then I'd actually be more comfortable sleeping in a hotel."

She laughed. "Me, too, buddy, but there isn't a hotel anywhere near Charity. It's like that town in *Children of the Corn*—once you're in, there's no way out."

Pictures of possessed kids with farm tools filled his mind. *Cripes.* This kept getting crazier and crazier. He readjusted on the hard plastic seat, trying desperately to get comfortable. There had to be something or somebody who was reasonable in Charity, otherwise this mission wouldn't get off the ground. At least, not with him anywhere near it. "Tell me more about your dad. He's retired Army. He's a farmer. What else?" Surely this was a man whom Carter could relate to.

She drank more coffee as she thought, her facial expressions indicative of someone who was struggling to come up with something to say. Maybe she didn't know the man all that well, considering his lengthy military career.

"My dad's a pretty straight shooter. His name is Harry. But you'll never call him that. Just Mr. Bell. He's big on respect. Um, he likes his animals and his land. He's up early." Carter homed in on another commonality. *Early risers get the worm.* "He likes order," she continued. *Nothing wrong with that.* "He collects semiautomatic weapons." Okay, that was a little disconcerting. "And he heads up the Charity Doomsday Preppers."

Carter blinked a couple times. "Doomsday? You mean those people who think the end of the world is near?"

She nodded, drank again, her lips smacking as she finally said, "Yep. They have a bunker up behind the post office, where they stockpile nonperishables, and they run drills once a month. They dress in camo, put the town on lockdown, and simulate an invasion."

"What kind of invasion?"

"Zombies," she said, straight-faced.

He sat back and sighed. The Bells might be certifiably crazy, this one included.

Things had gone from bad to worse.

"Just kidding." She grinned. "They're way more worried about the liberal government than zombies. Doesn't mean they wouldn't shoot anything that looked threatening, though."

My God. He wasn't going to survive. "Bell, I think I…"

"Jillian. If you call me Bell, they'll flip. I mean, nobody's going to shoot you over that, but they'll think the worst about you as a man—'no bringing up.' You need to call me by my God-given name or ..." Her lips clamped shut suddenly.

"Or what?"

She made a face and mumbled, "Or my nickname." She looked pained.

"I take it it's bad," he said.

"Just call me Jillian."

"Jillian." He said it slow and low to buy some time, but he liked the way it felt on his lips. And liking it didn't help him feel anymore settled about this. "I'm getting nervous here. These people sound a little ... off, and you aren't exactly straight with me. Part of me thinks they won't be as bad as you say, and part of me thinks they'll be worse." He flattened his hands on the table and braced himself. *If you're going to back out man, back out now.* "Actually, the more I think about it, the more I think..."

"I'll be straight with you. My nickname is Jillie. Some of them call me 'little Jillie,' which is way worse. It's always rubbed me the wrong way. And as far as the people being off, they are, but who isn't? I mean they aren't as bad as they sound. Unless you're me and you've ... done things to make a name for yourself." She looked away. "Then everybody sits around and waits for you to do something even dumber."

Like bring her football coach to a baptism and pass him off like he was her boyfriend? No, he couldn't see anything going wrong there.

The waitress returned, and Jillian greenlighted a fourth cup of coffee. It was like she had no "off" switch, no barometer to tell when enough was enough.

She stirred sugar into a fresh cup of coffee, and he noticed her shaky exhale. Her cheeks were red, too. Was she that embarrassed about a nickname? Or was it the idea of people waiting on her next mistake? Interesting. That devil-may-care attitude she wore like armor had a few cracks.

"One thing I can't figure out," he said. Jillian glanced at him over the rim of her cup. "You don't seem like the kind of person who should care what anybody thinks, so why does this matter so much? Is it your sister? The two of you are really close?"

Like she had last night in his car, she fidgeted and struggled with his silence until she spilled. "Wendy doesn't judge the things I do. She doesn't always like them, but she doesn't let them come between us either."

He could say the same thing about Amanda and how she'd handled his enlistment.

Stretching a hand across his forehead, he rubbed his temples. He could relate to a lot of this. Being the disappointment. Navigating those hostile waters alone. It hadn't been easy. But he got through. He could help Jillian get through, too.

Carter straightened. A successful mission could only have one leader. And as much as she liked calling the shots, it couldn't be her. She was too emotionally vested. So ... the first order of business would be to convince her to follow *his* lead—let him talk first. That way he could steer her clear of trouble. He would give the orders; she would listen. A patriarchal community like Charity would appreciate that. And while Jillian wouldn't like it at first, she'd be thankful once they were back in Cleveland and she'd had a peaceful visit with her nephew.

"Okay. We're doing this my way, now." He emphasized it with a sharp nod of his head. "We will stay over Saturday night so you're on time for the service, but we will not be staying over on Sunday. Get out quick before the shit hits the fan. You catch me?" She opened her mouth to protest, but he raised a hand to silence her. "My way will keep you out of trouble. That's what you want, isn't it?"

Her lips twisted, but then she nodded. Slowly. It looked like it hurt her a hell of a lot to relinquish the reins.

He reached into his pocket and pulled out his phone. "Now, let's go back over names so I can take them down to study later." He opened a new "note." When he looked up, she shocked him with an easy smile. It wrinkled the skin around her sparkling eyes and drew him in like a tractor beam.

"You're really going to do this, aren't you?" she asked. "You're really not going to run away."

"Of course I'm going to do this. I'm a man of my word."

Her mouth twisted. "Well, everybody breaks their word sometime. Everybody says they're going to do something and then they don't follow through. And I could tell a couple minutes ago, you were very close to backing out. So ... why are you really helping me? Don't give me that clichéd crap."

What she said was all true. Since he'd been five years old, he'd told everyone that he was headed for the NFL, and he never followed through. He could tell her about the time he backed out of that and what it did to his family, but he hesitated. It wasn't something he liked to share. And sharing it with her seemed unnecessarily intimate. They were already crossing lines. Lying to her family? Playing a couple? Spending the night in the same house? The whole thing left a bad taste in his mouth. So he settled on the one reason that would pass the smell test with his father.

"I'm helping you because it will give me leverage when it comes to the team. You're going to owe me—big time—after this."

She wrinkled her nose, making her freckles look extra cute. "You make it sound like I'll be your slave." The minute she said it, her eyes widened and her lips curled.

"Oh, you will be," he countered. When her jaw dropped, he smiled. "On the field, Bell."

She laughed, but the pink lingered on her cheeks. He stared into her happy eyes a little too long. What an interesting character.

His phone rattled against the table with an e-mail notification, and the noise broke his trance. The little moment of clarity allowed him to get back on track. "Names," he said.

Jillian listed the names of her immediate family members again. Then moved on to extended family and friends.

"Jodelle Prince is my sister's best friend and the godmother. Bob's cousin, David, is the godfather. Bob's parents, Dick and Betty, will be there. Bob's brother, Bruce. Bob's Uncle Merle." He couldn't type fast enough. "My cousins Roni, Johnnie, Olivia, and Pearl will probably make the drive. They're the only family who live close enough to attend. Johnnie is married, so his wife Lisa will be there. The neighbors at the end of the street, Alice and Skip—they're my parents' best friends, and..." she finally took a breath—a very big breath, "the preacher and his new wife."

The preacher. Carter looked at her. "What's *his* name?"

"Keller Winters. Everybody calls him Reverend Kel, except me. I don't call him anything out loud." She smiled, and it was honestly a little scary. "But in my head, I call him lots of things."

Carter could only imagine. Whatever had gone down between the couple left Jillian permanently scarred. He glanced at the tattoo. And yet the breakup had been a long time ago. Jillian definitely seemed happy to be free of him. Maybe Keller Winters wasn't someone Carter needed to be on high alert around. "What does the reverend call you?"

Jillian stared off into space. "Well, last time I saw him, he called me Jezebel, lost soul, and wayward woman. I'm sure he'll have some inspired new ones this time."

We'll see about that. Carter wasn't keen on getting lippy with a man of God, but if the guy was tough on Jillian, thereby threatening the mission, then Carter would be tough on him.

"He'll probably grill you, too," Jillian said. "Maybe even more than my parents."

"Grill me how?"

"The usual stuff. Where you work. Where you live. Your family. Your religion. How we met."

"How did we meet?"

"What do you mean? You're my coach. We met through the team."

"Won't that look bad? I mean, I'm sort of your boss; you're sort of my employee."

She scoffed. "If I walk in there looking too perfect, they're going to know something's up. I need to keep some of it real. Plus, it'll be easier for us to stick with the story if it's true. We met at practice, instant attraction. I thought you looked like Thor. You were mesmerized by my skill. I brought laughter to your gloomy world. You brought order to mine. Blah, blah, blah. We fought our feelings for as long as we could, telling ourselves we were all wrong for each other, but then bam! We couldn't keep our hands off each other anymore, and we decided we're adults who aren't hurting anyone, so why not explore the chemistry?"

Sounded eerily reasonable—except for that one little nugget … "You think I look like Thor?"

She slapped a hand over her mouth and shook her head wildly. "I'm just building a background here." But she couldn't keep a straight face.

He grinned. "You think I look like Thor." At that point, he may have puffed out his chest.

She tossed a wadded up napkin at him. "Concentrate. There's one small adjustment we have to make in order to make it sound completely legit. We met in February when indoor practices started. Got it?" A residual chuckle escaped her lips.

Cute as hell. But while he admired her, he did the math, and the two months they were supposed to be dating didn't seem like enough for him to be meeting the parents. "Nope. I veto that. We met last season."

And just like that, she was staring him down. "Why?"

"Because I'm in charge of this mission." Again, she didn't look impressed. "Jillian, think about it. You're not going to take me home after only knowing me for two months."

"Yes, I would. I totally would. Look at me." She lifted a strand of blue hair and pointed to the tattoos. "I'm impulsive." She said it like it was the most exciting word in the world.

"Well, I'm not impulsive." He felt his lip hitch. "*I* wouldn't go home with you after two months. Do you want this to be believable, or do you want to do it your way?"

She rolled her eyes. "Whatever."

He flashed a victorious smile. "Excellent. Now tell me what you do outside football."

"I party."

He ignored her attempt to rile him. "What do you do to earn a paycheck?"

"I party," she said again. "I'm a band promoter, which means I get paid to listen to live music and party. I'm promoting three bands right now: FOEbic, they're alt punk; ChixDigIt, they're eighties; and Chaos in the Castle, they're hard rock. I have them all booked regularly with guaranteed monies, which is beast mode in my business." She blew on her fingernails and then shined them on her shirt.

He could see her being very successful in that business. "Cool."

She eyed him skeptically. "Do you really mean that, or are you just trying not to seem so lame?"

Ouch. But, hey, she thought he looked like Thor. He chuckled. "I'm serious. Believe it or not, I'm a music fan. I used to be pretty into the indie scene. Ever hear of Harvey Danger?"

"Uh, yeah. They're one of the most underrated bands of their time."

"Yep."

Again, she regarded him with skepticism. "Let me guess, you know their one mainstream hit, 'Flagpole Sitta,' because it was in *American Pie.*"

He shook his head. "Nope. I bought the *Where Have All the Merrymakers Gone?* album on the recommendation of a friend. I like 'Carlotta Valdez' way better than 'Flagpole.'" He wasn't a singer, so he didn't try. Instead, he simply spoke his favorite lyrics from the song.

Jillian's jaw dropped.

"Surprised, huh?"

"Shocked." She pushed her coffee cup away and set her elbows on the table. "Did you know Sean Nelson released a solo album not too long ago?"

"I didn't." He'd kind of lost touch with that side of himself over the last few years. "I'll have to check it out."

She smiled. He smiled, too. A zap of connection traveled between them. They really did have some strange things in common.

"Have you heard of the Buzzcocks?" Fresh challenge in her voice.

He choked out a laugh. "Nice name. And no. I'm assuming they're a band."

She nodded. "They're a seventies punk band. Way, way before my time. Closer to yours, so I thought maybe you'd know them." She smirked.

Smart ass. "How old are you?" He should know that, too.

"Twenty-six."

"Baby," he said.

"Baby, my ass." She leveled him with a slow, sultry stare. "I could teach you a few things."

He bet she could. But ... they were getting off track. Again. "For this mission, I'm the teacher, sweetheart. And don't you forget it."

For the second time in a matter of minutes, he'd made her jaw drop, which was oddly satisfying. He made a mental note to do it again. If things kept going like this, spending the day with her in Charity wouldn't be so bad. In fact, it might be more fun than he'd had in a long time.

But first, he had to clear it with his dad.

• • •

Carter flagged his father down outside the stadium. *Just tell him the plan.* Helping Jillian was helping the team. His father should see that, too.

"Evening," his father said. Clipboard under his arm. The net full of freshly pumped-up footballs rested on his shoulder. All business.

Carter fell into step beside his him. "Question." He cleared his throat. "Can you cover for me at films on Sunday?"

His father looked at him. The slight hitch of his upper lip had Carter's nerves rolling again.

"Why?" his dad asked. "Sunday film was your brainchild."

Lie to him. Carter's running shoe caught on the pavement, and he stumbled. Where the hell had that bad advice come from? There were already enough lies attached to this mission. "I think I've figured out a way to rein in Bell once and for all."

His father looked very interested. "Have you now?"

Carter nodded. "Remember how she asked for permission to miss films? Well, she asked because she needs to go home for her nephew's christening, but she isn't enthusiastic about going. There are problems there. My gut tells me that's part of the reason she's been acting up lately. If she can get through this weekend without incident, she'll settle down. And if I help her with that, then she'll owe me. I'll have more leverage on the field."

His father shook his head. "We're football coaches, Carter, not family therapists."

"I know that, but I'm worried she'll go home and have a bad experience, and then she'll come back worse. We'll pay the price."

His father nodded in agreement. "I know it sounds crazy, Dad, but I really think if I go with her, as an ally and someone to help her through any rough patches, she'll thank me by working harder later."

His father stopped and looked at Carter with a face full of concern. "I don't know. It sounds like an awfully personal thing to do."

Carter nodded. "Think of it like a chaperone, someone to keep her out of the kind of trouble that will have repercussions on this team. You know?"

His father's brow hitched skeptically. "She's a little old to be needing a chaperone."

"Dad, when you offered me this position, you asked me to instill discipline in this offense and to get through to her as fast as possible. That's all I'm trying to do."

It sounded like a convincing argument to Carter, but his father still looked disgusted. "I'm not convinced. But if this is what you feel you have to do, then..." His father looked away and shook his head. "Do it." The man walked on.

Carter waited a few steps. Ten years ago, if they'd had a conversation about joining the Marines, would it have ended up like this—him practically begging to gain his father's reluctant permission? Or would he have been given the ultimatum he'd feared so much and expected?

"I want a full report when you get back," his father said over his shoulder.

"Yes, sir."

"And keep it on the down low. I don't want anyone getting the wrong idea or claiming favoritism."

Good point, especially since they were posing as boyfriend and girlfriend.

Carter swallowed the unrest. *It's a mission, man.* All missions were uncomfortable to a certain extent. *You'll get through it.* Just like he'd gotten through every other one.

Jillian Bell couldn't wreak more havoc than a hillside insurgence. At least he hoped not.

Chapter Seven

The bad news? Jillian was late. Again. She slammed her car door and raced across the parking lot. The good news? She'd booked FOEbic at Groll's bar for a regular "after hours" Saturday night gig. Normally, the high from that would've canceled out the panic of being late. Hell, normally she didn't panic, but Carter was doing her a huge favor, and ...

Oh, screw it! Things happened. So what? She was late. Carter could get over it. He could make her run laps. Big fucking deal.

Her phone buzzed in her hand with another text from Wendy and picture of Caleb. She gave it a quick glance and a smile that faded when she thought maybe Carter wouldn't get over her being late this time. Maybe he would actually be mad enough to cancel the trip to Charity.

Jillian busted into the empty locker room with a growl and dressed.

Her pants were untied, and her shoulder pads were crooked beneath her jersey, but she grabbed her helmet off the bench and then sprinted out the door again.

Everyone else was already stretching. They spread out over the field in an orderly fashion like the good little football players they were. The coaching crew stood around them—all except for Carter, who was on the warning track, looking ominously at her.

Her pulse rate, which was already elevated because of the running, soared.

"You're running until I tell you to stop!" Carter yelled.

"I know!" she yelled back. Then she took off around the track without another word.

Her steps felt heavy. Her head hurt. How mad would he have to be to back out?

"Bell, I know you're faster than that. Move!" he yelled.

She sucked it up and increased her pace, breathing hard through the stabbing pain in her right side. *You booked a gig*, she told herself. *Focus on that.* But she kept sneaking peeks of Carter's sullen face. His eyes narrowed as she passed. And she had the foreign impulse to mouth an apology. She bit her tongue instead. This trip home was totally messing with her head.

Three laps later, he motioned for her to join the rest of the team for stations. Blocking came first, which was good. She really needed to hit something.

"Where were you?" Tanya asked as they stood in line.

"Groll's."

Tanya bobbed her brows. "Was it business or pleasure?"

"Business. I booked FOEbic, then I got stuck in traffic."

Tanya scrunched her face. "Really? That's a lot more boring than I would've expected from you. I mean..."

Coach blew his whistle, cutting Tanya off and moving her up to the line. Jillian exhaled, happy to be off the discussion hook. But when they switched stations, MJ jogged up beside her. "Everything okay?"

"Fine. I got stuck in traffic."

"You should leave earlier." MJ grinned.

"Thanks, Captain Obvious."

"Bell!"

Crap. She turned her head to see Carter motioning for her to come to the sidelines. Would he tell her on-field that Charity was out? Whatever. She squared her shoulders and lifted her chin. But her legs felt heavy and her pulse hitched.

When she reached him, his expression hardened. "I don't appreciate being taken advantage of." His voice was low and intimidating. It was also disturbingly sexy.

She did not want to be thinking anything positive about him right now, so she straightened her back and shored her defenses.

"This wasn't about *you*. This was about my job. Some of us actually have to do all the work ourselves. We can't push it off on peons."

His eyes bulged. "I don't care what it was about. And you will talk to me with respect." He leaned closer. "Just because I agreed to help you off the field doesn't mean you can push the boundaries on field."

Ooh, she wanted to tell him to go screw himself, but again a faint—and rare—voice of reason told her to apologize. She growled instead. "Whatever. Just say you won't help me out this weekend. I know that's what you want to do. Get it over with. I'm in the middle of practice." She started to back away.

Though his expression was hard, his voice was surprisingly soft. "I'm not going to say that. I made you a promise. I follow through. Now, it's your turn. Practice time didn't change. Traffic patterns didn't change. If something work-related popped up, you either needed to take care of it well before practice, or if that wasn't possible and it truly was an emergency, you needed to text me or my dad. Is that so hard?"

She looked at the cloudless sky and exhaled. "Probably not."

"Jillian, look at me."

She did if only because hearing her first name on the football field was a bit startling.

"I'm not like other people who run away when you push them away. You push me, and I push back. Eventually one of us will break." He wore the faintest smile.

Nice sentiment, but the number of people who didn't run away from her could be counted on one hand. He didn't know enough about her to make a claim like that.

So why did a big part of her want to believe him?

She shrugged it off and chalked it up to the haze he created in her head with his smile. The bigger issue here was he thought he could break her.

Poor baby. He was delusional.

...

"I'm never driving with you again." Jade held out a hand. "Look at this. I'm shaking."

Jillian laughed as she swung open the front door of Pop's Gym & Ring. "You're exaggerating."

"I told you to stick with me," MJ said. "She's a terrible driver."

Jillian rolled her eyes. "I am not."

"You ran a red light, rolled through two stop signs, and ignored the 'no right turn on red' sign," Jade said.

"In all of those cases, no one was coming. The coast was clear for me to proceed."

"No! That's not how it works. Rules of the road aren't negotiable."

Jillian scoffed. "All rules are negotiable."

They wove through the people and equipment toward the back of the gym. Tanya was already ringside. "Who's taking me on first?" she yelled above the noise.

Jade shook her head. "Not me. Back and traps tonight." Jade was a hobby bodybuilder, but Jillian had a hunch the ring intimidated her. Once you stepped in, all eyes were on you, and Jade always said her five-ten height attracted enough attention.

MJ walked around the ring to talk to Terrell, who had stepped in to run the place when he and Tanya's father remarried their mother last year. That left Jillian free for sparring.

Tanya's challenging eyes landed on her.

"You're on." She nodded at Tanya and headed off to wrap her hands for optimal punching power and injury prevention. She needed both anytime she stepped into the boxing ring with Tanya Martin.

When Jillian finally split the ropes and climbed in, Tanya was ready, bouncing on the balls of her feet. "I've been looking forward to this all day! Ever since some mouthy tenth grader told me my gym classes were for sissies. Since I can't hit him, I'll settle for you." She slammed her padded fists together and Jillian cringed.

"Geez. Don't kill me. I've been punished enough for one day."

Tanya gave her the same squinty-eyed look she'd given her back at the field when she'd witnessed Jillian and Carter's sideline conversation. "Mmm hmm. And just what is the deal with you and Thor?"

Jillian closed her eyes briefly to prepare an answer, and *bam*! Tanya jumped in with, "Girl, you better not be messin' with his hammer."

"Whoa! What?" MJ was ringside now, staring up at them like she couldn't believe what she'd heard.

"No!" Jillian looked each of them straight in the eye. "Hell no. You saw him pull me aside today, but you couldn't hear him ream me out. Honest to God, at one point I wanted to take his hammer and shove it up his ..."

"We get the picture." Tanya was bouncing even faster now. "But you know what they say. There's a fine line between love and hate, and you two have been hatin' on each other a lot these past two weeks."

"Did he rescind his permission for you to miss films on Sunday?" MJ asked.

Jillian's chest tightened. This was getting too close to the truth. "No."

Tanya stopped moving. "What *aren't* you saying?"

"Nothing. Can we just box?" She shuffled forward.

MJ gasped. "Something *is* going on between you and Thor."

"No! Nothing!" They looked at her like she was the worst liar in the world. "Nothing like *that*," she corrected.

"Then like what?" Tanya was in her face now.

Jillian dropped her arms to her sides and exhaled loudly. "Fine! You guys win. You said I couldn't behave long enough to make it through an entire day in Charity, and I guess I must've let you get to me, because, well, I ended up asking Carter to come with . . to keep me in line. It just sort of came out the night he helped me with the battery, and it snowballed into this whole charade where he's going to pretend to be my boyfriend."

"Oh my God." MJ's mouth didn't close after she said the words.

"He said yes to something that stupid?" Tanya asked.

Jillian nodded.

"Why would he say yes?" MJ looked confused.

"Girl, you better start moving again, so I can hit you without feeling guilty," Tanya said.

Jillian hit gloves with Tanya to show the match had begun and started shuffling side to side. "It's no big deal."

MJ kept talking from her spot on the floor. "He's our coach! You can't blur the lines like that. It's completely inappropriate."

Tanya threw a punch, and Jillian stepped back to make space. Nothing but air.

"There's nothing inappropriate about it." Jillian moved in and landed a couple punches. But she had to backpedal immediately.

Quick as she was, Tanya caught her in the jaw. Jillian shook off the sting.

"You're both crazy," Tanya said.

"No, we aren't. I'm doing this because I need someone who sees the world as rigidly as my parents do to help me navigate the visit. He's doing it because it'll give him leverage on the football field, like I'll listen more and respect him because I'll be so grateful. Okay, maybe that part's crazy, but all in all, I think our reasons are solid. He's really and truly not my type. I promise you." Jillian jabbed.

Tanya dodged. "Maybe you're his type. Maybe he likes a project. I mean, why would a guy agree to something like that if he wasn't interested in the girl? And don't give me that crap about leverage on the field. He could just threaten to bench you."

Jillian laughed at that, because he already had. Then she laughed harder at the idea of her being Carter's type. "Are you kidding me? Most of the time, I think he wants to drop-kick me."

"So how are you going to get through two days together without him drop-kicking you?" MJ asked.

Jillian considered that and paid for the distraction with a pop in the ribs. She winced. "*I'm* not going to Charity. A cleaned-up version of me is going to Charity. Thor won't want to drop-kick Jillie—nobody will." She hoped.

Jillian landed a love tap on Tanya's shoulder.

"Weak," Tanya said.

"I am completely against people changing themselves to fit in." MJ rattled on about self-love and acceptance. Then she circled back around to the team. "I mean, all the talks I've given to young girls and women about owning who they are, like we're supposed to own who we are as full-tackle football players, and here I am listening to one of my best friends go against everything I preach. Everything! And you of all people." She grabbed her head and groaned. "Jillian, make them love you for who you are or not at all, rather than reduce our team to Match.com."

Finally Tanya threw up her hands. "Please, can we just shut up about it? Jill and I will settle it in the ring."

"T..." Jillian dropped her arms again and stopped shuffling her feet. "There's nothing to settle. It's not the big deal MJ is making it out to be."

"Until somebody gets hurt." Tanya's brows pulled together atop her nose. "You keep shooting from the hip like this, and one of these, days you're going to lose the whole damn joint. You catch me?"

Not really, but Jillian kept her mouth shut.

"The impulsiveness is going to get you into big trouble," Tanya continued. "The kind of trouble you won't be able to get out of."

Jillian doubted that. She was pretty slippery. And to prove it, she dodged Tanya's punch and landed one of her own.

The rest of the match was silent except for grunts and heavy breathing. In the end, it was hard to tell who won. They were both dripping messes. In their exhaustion, some kind of understanding passed between their eyes.

"It'll be fine," Jillian said.

Tanya nodded. "Just remember, he's not your usual conquest. You're completely different people, and completely different people want completely different things. If those lines get blurred somehow, it will end badly."

Jillian smiled. "But it won't, because he's not a conquest."

Tanya didn't look convinced. "I know you, girl. Everything's a conquest. Just please be careful with this one."

Tanya split the ropes and dropped to the floor. Jillian followed behind her.

MJ was there waiting, looking hella concerned, but she tossed an arm around Jillian's shoulder and said, "Okay. I've had some time to think about all of this. I know how hard it's going to be for you to go home after the way you left Wendy's wedding. I understand that part, but I'm worried taking Carter Howl along for the ride will only cause more trouble. And what if that trouble comes back to Cleveland with you? It could hurt the team. It could hurt you."

Jillian shook her head. "That's not going to happen. I promise. I have to be on my best behavior for this weekend to work, and believe me, Thor's not going to tolerate anything less." She squeezed MJ's hand. "This time, there's a method to my madness."

Chapter Eight

Two hours after the Clash had put the beat down on an injury-thinned Detroit team, Jillian gave herself a good, hard look in the bathroom mirror. She wore a pale, yellow-knit twinset and black cigarette pants just this side of respectable. On her feet were patent leather Mary Janes. Around her neck were the pearls her parents gave her for high school graduation. The blue streaks in her hair had been dyed brown to match her natural color.

Sellout, the voice in her head said.

I am not selling out. I'm surviving. And she was compromising for the sake of her sister and nephew. There would be no repeat of the notorious wedding day.

She unplugged the curling iron and headed back to her bedroom to finish packing. Carter would be here soon. On that thought, her stomach tied in knots. Was she really going to be able to survive hour upon hour with him, let alone convince her family they were a couple?

Too bad Charity was a dry town. It could be a very long couple of days.

For a split second, she contemplated filling a few empty hairspray bottles with vodka just to get her through. Then again, booze hadn't made the wedding any easier. She shoved the impulse aside and loaded her suitcase with the pile of conservative clothes Jade had pulled out before heading off on another blind date her mother had cooked up in the hopes of marrying her off to a Korean.

There was a big height difference between Jade and Jillian, but some of the items might work. The cardigan sweaters were good for covering her tattoos, and the longer length meant they would cover her ass, too. She packed those. Then she stared at the floral tank dress hanging on her closet door. A red knit shrug hung over the dress and matched the roses covering the bodice and puff-n-pleat white skirt. Very virginal. So not Jillian.

But that was the whole point of this weekend, wasn't it?

She rid her makeup bag of too much gray and black and added the pastel colors Jade had given her just as Carter knocked on her apartment door. She stole one last look at the stranger reflected back at her in the entryway mirror. *Showtime, Jillie.* Then she took a deep breath and opened the door.

"Hey ... oh ... wow." He stood outside her apartment taking in the transformation.

"Your hair," he said almost reverently. "It's so..." he reached out and touched the very tip of one of her spiral curls, "springy and shiny."

She threaded her fingers through the hair at her crown. For someone who air-dried as a rule, the results of actually spending time on her hair were astounding. "It was all Jade's idea. She made me use some oil stuff that smells like coconuts." She leaned forward briefly so he could sniff.

He just looked at her funny.

"What? Don't you like coconuts?" she asked.

"No. It's good. It's ... all good." He smiled. "I guess I'm just a little surprised you're talking this so seriously."

"Of course I'm taking it seriously. I'm taking you, aren't I?" And she was surprisingly glad she was. He looked every bit the part in his khaki pants and lightweight, three-quarter zip sweater. The soft blue shade made his eyes pop, and for a minute, her brain blanked while she stared into them. *Excellent.* She hoped that was exactly what happened with the people in Charity. Hypnosis by hottie. Then she would have room to breathe.

They hit the road with the music blaring. He turned it down. She turned it up. At one point, she covered the console, but he had controls on the steering wheel.

"Would you crank Harvey Danger?" she asked.

"No, I wouldn't. I don't like any music that loud."

"Well, if it's too loud, then you're too old." She laughed and turned up the radio again, bouncing to the beat. Who didn't like loud music? She turned it down again. "Wait, what else don't you like? I don't think we covered this."

"I don't like fish."

"In aquariums or on your plate?"

"Plate."

"Yeah, me neither. Don't worry. My family is very meat and potatoes. Anything else?"

He propped his left elbow on the car door and snatched his sunglasses from an overhead compartment. Damn he looked good in the black Ray-Ban aviators.

"Carbs. I eat high protein. But I'm pretty adaptable. Even if they put nothing but a loaf of bread and a piece of fish in front of me, I'd eat it and make them think it was the greatest thing in the world. Chameleons survive in the desert."

Another military reference, she was sure. God, her dad was going to love this. She settled in for the ride but didn't touch the radio again. In fact, she barely took her eyes off of him. They talked. They laughed, and the two hours flew by until she saw the sign reading "Charity: A Little Piece of Heaven." That quieted her.

The knots were back, and she pressed a hand against her stomach. She could do this. She could behave for two damn days. And if she started slipping, Thor would wield his hammer.

"Right at the Methodist church."

Her parents' farm was still several miles away. She fought the urge to roll down the windows and turn up the music again, fill the air with something more exciting than the sound of birds and locust.

"One more time," Carter said. "Your parents are Karen and Harry, but Mr. and Mrs. Bell as far as I'm concerned—no first names. Your sister is Wendy. Her husband is Bob. Their son is Caleb. The rest of them I'll worry about after we've been introduced." He glanced at her. "You and I met last football season. Everything else is real. My job. Your job. Our friends and family."

"Easy peasy," she said.

But a thick silence followed.

Again, she itched to turn up the music, and a sudden urge to take the wheel gripped her. She'd burn down the mile-long dirt road that led to her parents' farm kicking up clouds of fury behind her like she had when she'd left town after breaking off her engagement. Oh the freedom she'd felt! But she couldn't do that now, mostly because there was no way in hell Carter would relinquish the wheel. She craved one little drink to banish the edge.

"By the way, Charity is a dry town," she said.

His jaw pulsed when he hit a rut in the road. "No alcohol sold or no alcohol allowed, period?"

"No alcohol allowed, period." But there were ways to get it in.

He hit another rut and groaned.

She knew exactly how he felt.

When they finally pulled up in front of the big white farmhouse, five people filed onto the front porch. She saw her mother first, complete with apron and dishtowel, then her father, who was surprisingly dressed in something other than overalls. Her smiling sister, with a bundle of baby in her arms, and her disapproving brother-in-law were there, too. Seeing Wendy look so happy smoothed out some of the wrinkles in Jillian's belly.

"Here goes nothing," Carter said beneath his breath.

Here goes everything, she thought.

She was suddenly so grateful he was here that she reached across the center console and squeezed his hand.

Something hot and strong shot up her arm, settling her heartbeat.

He pulled his hand away, put the car in park, and faced her. He looked nervous as hell. "I think I better follow your lead."

She nodded. "Unless my lead ... goes out of control. Then you take the lead until I calm down. Got it?" She tossed him an anxious smile and pushed out of the car.

Everyone on the porch stood stock still, staring at her like she was a stranger, staring at the car like it was a spaceship. She smoothed a hand over her jumpy stomach and said, "I'm here."

That seemed to snap at least one of them out of it.

"Jillie!" Wendy passed the bundled-up baby to Bob and scurried off the porch with her arms open. "Oh, my goodness. Look at you! You're so beautiful!"

Jillian wrapped her arms around her sister and buried her face in her strawberry-scented hair—the same shampoo they'd used as kids. Childhood memories flooded her, and she closed her eyes, blocking everyone else out. "I missed you," she whispered.

Wendy broke the hug and grabbed Jillian's hands. "Not anymore, because you're here." She squealed. "And you aren't alone!"

"Who's your young man, Jillie?" The deep voice made her let go of her sister's hands and stand straighter.

Her father had stopped a few feet away from a surprisingly calm-looking Carter.

"Oh!" A little enthusiasm would hide her supreme nervousness, so she smiled brightly. "Everyone ..." she said, "this is Carter Howl, my ... boyfriend."

Even though she'd practiced saying it in the mirror, the word still sounded so ridiculous it formed on a giggle. She scrambled to Carter's side, grabbed his arm, pulled him closer, and planted a kiss on his cheek to hide her incriminating reaction. Then she dropped down to the heels of her feet and watched him shake her father's hand.

Surreal. All of it. So this was what it felt like to bring somebody home?

She licked her lips, tasting something spicy through her blueberry-flavored gloss. Probably Carter's aftershave. In the midst of the most nerve-wracking situation she'd ever been in, the heat of attraction crawled up the back of her neck. She licked her lips again. *Mm.* The taste of him did something to her, and she got caught up in the moment, standing taller and enjoying even more the way her sister was preening over him like he was a prized bull.

Jillian Mae had done something right this time.

"Welcome to Bluebell Farms," said a soft voice.

Jillian looked to the porch, where her mother slowly navigated the steps. There was pain on her face and an exaggerated hitch in her gait, which meant her rheumatoid arthritis was much worse than it had been two years ago. *Shit.* As much as Jillian didn't get on with her mother, she didn't want to see her like this.

"Mama," Jillian said, suddenly caring very little about what had happened last time between them.

As she folded her mother into a stiff hug, she noticed how Bob stayed with the baby on the porch. He was going to make her go to him. Typical Bob.

Carter introduced himself to her mother, while Wendy tugged on Jillian's elbow.

"Come meet the baby," she said, coaxing Jillian toward the porch.

Bob stood stone-faced.

"Caleb, this is your Aunt Jillie." Wendy moved the blanket away from his face.

Jillian stepped closer and ignored Bob. She stole a peek at her nephew, who was wrapped in a yellow blanket. Pink skin. Tiny nose. And the longest lashes she'd ever seen. "Oh my God, he's gorgeous."

"Oh my *goodness*," her mother corrected from somewhere behind her.

Jillian closed her eyes for a brief second, grinding her teeth. It was a good reminder that she couldn't for a minute let down her guard and think this was going to be easy.

"Would you like to hold him?" Wendy asked.

"Not now. He's napping," Bob said sternly. "Wendy, take him up to bed."

Jillian watched her brother-in-law hand off the child, and then he walked down the porch steps with a hand extended to Carter.

"You can help me," Wendy said.

But Jillian couldn't see how leaving Carter alone with the others was a good idea. "Next time," she said, and she bounded down the steps.

"That's some vehicle you got there," Bob said. "Flashy."

Jillian could tell by the pulse in Carter's jaw that he didn't like Bob—or his comment.

"Thank you," Carter said as gracious as ever, and she thought maybe she'd read him wrong. "It's not nearly as flashy as the Ferrari I was considering last week. Jillian talked me down from that ledge."

She held in her laugh. But a few seconds later, she nearly lost her composure when Carter slipped a hand to her neck. More heat. This time it ran all the way to her toes.

Now, didn't that just complicate things?

• • •

Bob was a dick. The guy looked at Jillian like she was gum on the bottom of his shoe, and that didn't sit right with Carter. As far as he could tell, Jillian was trying—hard—and her brother-in-law ought to be trying at least a little. Other than that, the family seemed reasonable. Wendy was off-the-charts happy to see Jillian, and Mr. and Mrs. Bell looked cautious but hopeful. He eyed up Mrs. Bell again. She moved slowly and stiffly, but between the winces of pain, he could see a resemblance to Jillian. The same mouth. The same nose. But her hair was gray, and her body was round. It made him wonder exactly what was wrong with her and how old she was, because her husband's head was covered in thick brown hair, and her daughter Wendy looked straight out of high school.

"Carter, we have coffee, iced tea, and lemonade. What can I get you? And for heaven's sake, sit." That's when he realized everyone but him and Mrs. Bell were gathered around the large kitchen table.

"Lemonade, please," he said, taking his hands out of his pockets and noting the empty seats.

Bob looked at him funny. He'd been looking at him funny for the last twenty minutes. Maybe the guy had a feeling something was up between Carter and Jillian. Then again, maybe the guy always looked like a goof. But just in case, Carter bypassed the closest empty seat and sat beside Jillian. Then he stretched his arm over the back of her chair and smoothed his thumb over her shoulder. *Get a load of that, jackass.*

"Jillie, help your mother." Mr. Bell's booming command made Jillian's muscles twitch. "Your sister is busy with the baby."

Jillian glanced at Carter, a twisted look on her face, and then she nodded to her father and left her seat.

"So what do you deal in?" Bob asked.

What the hell did that mean? Was he insinuating that Carter was a drug dealer?

"You know, to afford a car like that," Bob added without shame.

Yep, big ol' Bob thought Carter was into something nefarious that yielded a lot of cash. Idiot. Carter smiled. "I deal in food I own thirty restaurants—nationwide."

"Anything we may have heard of?" Mr. Bell asked.

He hoped. They'd recently increased marketing efforts in Pennsylvania. Not that a dry town just across the border was their target, but if these people had access to radio and television, they should've heard the name. "Shock & Awe."

Bob looked smug again. "Boozing establishments."

"Carter is an ex-Marine." Jillian's off-topic announcement landed hard along with his lemonade.

He picked a napkin off the pile and swiped at the liquid that had spilled over the rim. "Former Marine," he corrected, still annoyed at Bob's last comment.

Jillian was already darting away from the table and back to the kitchen.

"You don't say? I'm retired Army," Mr. Bell said.

"I know. Jillian told me. It's something to be mighty proud of. Thank you for your service." It always meant so much when people thanked him.

Mr. Bell gave him a gracious nod. The respectful look that passed between them drove home at least one of the reasons Jillian had asked him here. The military thing had been her secret weapon.

"You ever kill anybody?" Bob asked.

If Carter weren't so shocked by the lack of tact, he would've glared at the man. Seriously, this guy was part of this family yet Jillian was the black sheep?

"Finally! I thought he'd never go down." Wendy interrupted the conversation, breezing past the table and into the kitchen to help the other women. "Oh!" She called over her shoulder. "I put your stopwatch back in your drawer."

Carter expected Mr. Bell to thank his daughter, but instead he caught a tight nod coming from Bob. Interesting. If the stopwatch and dresser were Bob's, then that meant Wendy and Bob lived in this house. *Freeloader.* The guy was an even bigger loser than Carter thought. And wait. What the hell did a stopwatch have to do with a baby's nap?

"So, how'd you meet my daughter?" Mr. Bell asked.

"He's one of the coaches on my football team." Jillian placed a stack of plates and silverware beside a platter of brown, sliced bread, and then she slipped back into the chair next him.

Nobody said anything, and for a moment, Carter wished they'd come up with something less morally ambiguous, but then good ol' Bob dropped another gem.

"I thought you said you dealt in booze. Now you're coaching football. Which is it?"

"Both," Carter said. "I'm the offensive coordinator for my father's team."

"That's nice," Wendy said. "You have football in common." She smiled sweetly, and Carter wondered how a good kid like that got messed up with such a jerk.

"I still don't get why any woman would want to play football," Mr. Bell said. "That's a man's sport."

Jillian straightened, and Carter calmed her down with a simple pat of his hand on her thigh. "Not anymore," Carter said. "There are twenty-seven teams in this league alone. More leagues pop up every day. And some youth football programs are actively recruiting girls. It's a brave new world," he said with a smile.

Bob grunted.

Beneath the table, Jillian patted Carter's thigh right back.

He smiled wider.

"Where did you serve while you were active duty?" Mr. Bell asked.

Carter watched him grab a slice of bread and butter it soundly. "Iraq. Twice."

"Your mother must've been worried sick," Mrs. Bell said as she sat. "Lord knows how much I worried about this man over the years." She looked at her husband, who didn't look back.

"I'm sure she would've been, ma'am, but my mother passed away before I enlisted."

"I'm sorry to hear that," she said. "Eat." The maternal tone in her voice reminded him a little bit of Amanda.

"Thank you." He took a slice of bread off the raised plate and was surprised to find it tasted sweet and literally melted in his mouth. "Delicious," he said to Mrs. Bell's supreme satisfaction.

"Do you love being a mother?" Jillian asked Wendy, and the conversation finally veered away from him.

He sat there quietly, enjoying his bread, despite the carbs, and missing his family.

"What's with the stopwatch?" Jillian asked.

"I time his feedings. Bob says a schedule is important. It establishes expectations."

Carter choked on his lemonade. Those exact same words—a schedule is important—had come out of his mouth thirty miles outside of town, when Jillian had asked to stop for a Coke and some chips. He instantly regretted having anything in common with Bob. He coughed into his napkin and made a mental note to ease up a little this weekend.

Mrs. Bell returned from another painful-looking kitchen run with a pitcher of fresh lemonade in her hand. He wondered why nobody seemed terribly concerned about her condition. "Mrs. Bell, please sit. We're good. This is all more than enough. No need to spoil us."

"It's not for us," Bob said. "Reverend Kel will be here soon."

Jillian's head spun around so fast a strand of hair whipped Carter in the cheek along with a noseful of its coconut scent. "What? Here? Why?"

"He wants to go over some things with Bob and me," Wendy said quietly, not making eye contact.

"He has an office at the church, doesn't he?" The sharp tone of Jillian's voice brought Carter right back to the early days of knowing her, the days when she'd made it clear she was capable of challenging anything and anybody.

"Don't get so ruffled about it," Bob said. "Good Lord knows the man's not coming to see you." The dick chuckled.

Jillian dug her fingernails into Carter's thigh, and he took it as an SOS. "There better not be a man coming to see my girl." He smoothed a hand awkwardly over her thigh beneath the table, and sucked a quick breath through his open mouth. There was probably something better he could've said.

"No worries there," Bob said, still wearing that ridiculous smile. "Rev. Kel wised up."

"What do you mean he wised up?" With a scraping sound, Jillian's butt hovered above her chair. Carter gripped just above her knee, hoping to settle—and sit—her down. "I broke up with him. I'm the one who wised up!"

"Jillian Mae," Mr. Bell boomed. "Sit. And don't start arguing about the past. Your choices were your choices. The reverend is welcome in this house anytime. He always has been."

Carter wanted to smack the grin off Bob's face, but instead, he focused on Jillian and how he could diffuse the situation.

She was staring stonily at her father. "Keller's always welcome, unlike me. Thanks for the reminder." Then she pushed away from the table and stormed out of the room.

Shit. Carter stood. "I'll, uh, just go check on her."

Chapter Nine

Jillian heard the dry grass crunch behind her, and she knew it was Carter. She'd bolted from the farmhouse enough times to know that nobody in her family would follow.

"Well, that didn't take long." She wrapped her arms around her waist and stared at the manmade runoff pond between the house and the barn.

"Bob's a dick," Carter said.

"He is. He really is." She faced him. "But he comes from a good family, and apparently he's a good worker for my dad, so the farm will go to him." Sarcastic bitterness tinged her voice. "Bob inherits everything."

Carter whistled. "Not your mother or sister or…" he smiled at her, "even you? Bet you'd look cute shoveling cow manure."

She softened and grinned. "I'll have you know I'd be an awesome farmer if that's what I wanted to do, but nope. Bob's the heir. If something happens to my father, Bob gets the house, the land, and the women. It's like some farm-fetish Jane Austen movie." She waved a hand. "You've probably never seen a Jane Austen movie, so never mind."

"Actually, I've seen a couple. My sister, Amanda, used to have a thing for Colin Firth."

"Most women do." Because Colin Firth was kind and respectful. He'd never invite his daughter's ex-fiancé into his house, knowing it would upset her.

"Why doesn't Bob like you?" Carter asked.

She faced the pond again. Water bugs skipped across the top. She'd told Carter she'd messed up at the wedding, but she hadn't told him to what extent. If that bomb got dropped while they were here, and Carter still didn't know, it might come as a shock to him, and that might give a lot of people satisfaction she didn't want them to have. "I had sex with his brother."

"Okay?" He didn't sound too impressed.

"Bob found us going at it in the janitor's closet at the wedding reception."

"Oh. Yeah. That makes a little more sense."

"It does. I was wrong. I admit that, but Bob blames me and only me, because I brought the booze." She glanced over her shoulder, figuring she'd find him looking disgusted or disappointed. That was usually the way the story was received, especially around here. Sure enough, he was frowning.

"Well, you crossed a serious line there. What were you thinking, Bell?" He shook his head, and the knots in her stomach intensified. "Booze at a wedding reception? You savage." Then he cracked that smile, the thousand-watt one that could instantly turn her knees to jelly.

She shook her head, smiling a little now. "Yeah, well, I guess only a booze dealer like you could understand."

He laughed, a booming sound that cut across the quiet valley, and Jillian laughed, too, feeling the remaining knots loosen. She tilted her head and surveyed his calm, casual demeanor.

"You know, you're being very diplomatic about this," she said, eyes narrowed. "But I'm sure inside you're all twitchy." He looked at her expectantly, and she nodded. "A guy like you takes one look at a girl like me and sees trouble."

He took more than one look at her. In fact, he stared at her for the longest time.

She stared right back, losing herself in those brilliant blue eyes, remembering the way a quick taste of his skin had lingered on her lips.

"I don't see trouble," he murmured, leaning closer.

The backdoor rattled, snapping her head around. But when she looked at the house, nobody was there.

"Maybe it was the wind," Carter said, snagging a strand of hair that had blown across her lips.

But there was definitely a shadow in the mudroom window, and the curtain twitched. "Bob," Jillian grimaced. "He's such a creeper." Then her heart slammed against her ribs when Carter slipped a hand to her waist and hauled her closer. "Wha ..."

"Let's give good ol' Bob something to really talk about."

Her eyes were still open when Carter's mouth lightly met hers. But when his arms slinked around her waist and he held her tighter against his hard body, instinct took over. It didn't matter where they were, who he was, or who was watching. He was a man with his lips on hers, and her body knew what to do.

She kissed him back, touching the tip of her tongue to the seam of his mouth, wrapping her arms around his neck and pulling him in. He opened for her, tangling his tongue with hers. She melted ... slipped away. And it was absolutely delicious.

But it couldn't last. Something buzzed by her ear, and she followed that annoying little noise on the wind until she picked up the sound of an approaching car. Keller was here.

She pulled back with one last lick of Carter's lips and blinked up at him. "Wow. That was ... unexpected." For a couple reasons. One, she couldn't believe he'd done it, and two, she couldn't believe it had felt so good. She used to tell Tanya kissing—*just* kissing—was boring, but this ... She touched her bottom lip.

"Just playing the part," he said, stepping back. But his eyes were twinkling. "I think Bob suspects something."

"Oh." So Carter was just being chivalrous. Of course, he was. "Then, I guess I should thank you for taking one for the team."

"Jillian ..."

The screen door on the back porch clanged open followed by her father's voice, "Reverend Kel and his wife are here, Jillian Mae. Come inside to greet our guests." The door clanged shut behind him, a very loud, very final period on his command.

She stared at the house. Her emotions were completely frayed. "You know, I don't have to go back in there. We could run to your car and drive home to Cleveland." She looked at him. "Pretend like none of this ever happened." Mind-blowing, confusing-as-hell kiss included.

"Is that what you want to do?"

Actually, what she wanted to do was duct tape Bob's ankles, wrists, and mouth and shove him in the basement root cellar. Then she might have a prayer of getting through this weekend.

She nodded. "I'd love to leave, but that's what they *expect* me to do, and if I do it, it's going to hurt Wendy again. So I'm staying."

Chin up, shoulders back, she marched across the backyard, wondering if her mother still kept duct tape in the basket by the door.

• • •

The Reverend G. Keller Winters didn't seem to be impressed with either Jillian's "conversion" or her "boyfriend." Maybe that was because he was too busy being so very impressed with himself. She returned him the same courtesy by yawning while he droned on and on.

"And I told those boys, 'Until the day he dies, you can guarantee your father will be catching the biggest fish. Father first. In all things.'"

His wife Anne, whom Jillian had never met before, sat sweetly by his side. Keller had introduced her as "the angel" he'd met while away on a mission trip. Then he made a point to praise her God-fearing nature and obedience. Anne looked about nineteen.

That could've been me, Jillian thought. And yet, she knew it wasn't true. Obedient was a four-letter word as far as she was concerned. Married or not. It wasn't in her nature.

She played with the sleeve of her sweater, folding it up just enough to show the blue tip of her Cinderella tattoo. Maybe she didn't always make the right decisions, but breaking off her engagement to Keller had been the rightest decision she'd ever made. No regrets. She'd heard he finally married someone young and impressionable last year, so maybe he didn't have any now either.

When Keller asked to "commune" with Bob and Wendy privately about their son's "spiritual journey," Jillian saw her chance for a reasonable escape. "I'm going to take Carter into town," she said.

Her mother looked at her father, and her father looked at the wall clock. "Everything's closed over there."

"I know, but it's still light, and I want to show him around. Tomorrow we won't have time." She looked at Carter. "You want to go, don't you?"

"Sure, but we'll need to be back before dark, otherwise I won't be able to find my way."

Big deal. "Then I'll drive."

"Not going to happen."

Her father chuckled. "Spoken like a wise man."

Anne didn't say a word.

The idea that Jillian's parents were somehow skeptical about her plan to go into town coupled with this idea that she wasn't fit to drive an expensive car was ridiculous. She opened her mouth to tell them all where they could go, but instead she closed it on the pitiful sight of her mother hobbling off toward the kitchen.

Once Jillian was inside Carter's car, she said her peace. "Tell me. What do my parents think we're going to do? Go off behind one of those closed buildings in town and drink from the stash in your trunk and then bang like rabbits in the backseat of your car." She tugged off her sweater in an agitated huff. "And this idea that I can't be trusted with your car. Please. I could change all four tires faster than you could find the auto parts store. You bet your sweet ass I'm capable of driving the damn thing."

Convinced she'd made her point, and feeling much better because of it, she dropped her head to the seat rest and closed her eyes. "I don't even want to go to town. Town is a decrepit ice cream parlor, a Dollar General, and Mel's Service Station. I just wanted to get the hell out of that house. Anne didn't say a damn word. She creeps me out."

"You mean we aren't going to get drunk and desecrate the backseat of my car?" He hit the steering wheel. "Then I'm turning around."

Laughter burst past her lips. His irreverent sense of humor shocked her.

She opened her eyes to see him smiling. He was just what she needed. Memories from the kiss swirled in her head as she smiled back at him. It had felt like they were doing more than playing a part, but what did she know? She probably laid claim to more drunken kisses than sober ones. Maybe that was why kissing Carter had felt so different ... so real.

"Hey, is your mom okay?" he asked.

The question sort of took her off guard.

"It's just hard not to notice how much pain she's in when she's walking around. And her hands," he added. "They're so swollen."

The words conjured an image in Jillian's head, and her shoulders slumped. "She has rheumatoid arthritis. It's obviously getting worse."

"I'm sorry to hear that," he said.

"Me, too," she said.

Jillian glanced out the window at the familiar landscape. How many times had she flown down this road looking for an escape? Back then, her mother had been strong enough to wield an umbrella or even throw a cookbook when Jillian had been mouthy. The crippled woman back at the house didn't look like she could make it up the stairs without someone spotting her. It was surprisingly worrisome—and depressing. If Jillian stayed away another two years, how bad would her mother be then? And what about Caleb, sweet Caleb? Wrapped in a blanket, sleeping peacefully, he hadn't looked like he was sick. And freaking Bob sure didn't cut the kid any slack because of a heart defect.

"What kind of man uses a stopwatch to time the feedings of a sick kid?" she asked.

Carter grunted. "A prick. I just might have to go stealth mode tonight and steal that thing." He glanced at her. "Poof! Nobody will ever see it again."

She grinned. "I like the way you think." It wasn't that far off from her own thoughts.

"So ... if we aren't going to town, then where would you like to go?" he asked.

There weren't many options in Charity. Fortunately, she'd spent the four years she'd been stuck here fleshing out the best spots to get away. And she knew just the place.

• • •

Much to Carter's dismay, Charity, Pennsylvania, loved its dirt. Every street except the main road was covered in it, every parking lot, too. And there wasn't a car wash in sight.

He tried to avoid the biggest ruts as he pulled into the lot Jillian had led him to. "Now I know why there are so many trucks around here."

"If you think this is bad, you should see it in the winter."

No, thanks. He pulled as far back as he could go, and then put the car in park. As soon as he did, a little hesitation settled in his chest. Why had she brought him here? After that microimplosion about getting drunk and having sex, an empty dirt lot surrounded by green space made him wonder. Maybe that kiss had given her the wrong idea. Hell, it had given him the wrong idea for a split second, too.

Carter smoothed a hand over his mouth and shoved those memories aside. He was not going to make more out of it than it was. He was not going to berate himself for taking the liberty in the first place. He was not going to rationalize it. He was not going to worry about it. He was just going to forget it. "So ... why are we here?"

"I thought you might like to see where I learned to play football."

He looked at the landscape again. He supposed he could make out the boundaries of a field, but they were faint, and large clumps of weeds sprung up every few feet. Maybe it had never been regulation. "This is a football field?"

"It used to be. Believe it or not, Charity had a football team when I moved here. But they didn't have a soccer team, which crushed me. I used to come out here whenever I needed to get away from home and kick my fluorescent yellow soccer ball until it was too dark to see where it landed. One day, the football coach saw me split the uprights, and he asked me to try it with a football. I did, and much to a lot of people's dismay, I kicked for the Charity Cherry Blossoms for two seasons, until the team folded because there weren't enough people to play."

Huh. It was a cool story. "So why aren't you kicking for our team?"

"Because I'm a better receiver." She grinned, and then she was out of the car.

With his door open and one foot on the gravel, he watched her walk onto the field. Without the prissy sweater, she looked more like the Jillian he knew. The little yellow tank top tucked into tight black pants showed off every curve and put her tattoos on display. They gave her interest and edge, and for some reason, that made him smile.

He popped his trunk, and at the sound, she turned.

"You *do* have booze in that trunk, don't you?"

"Better," he said slyly. And then he produced a football.

She whooped, kicked off her shoes, and then sprinted across the grass at full speed. Hair flying, lips flapping, arms waving overhead. "Hit me!" True blue Jillian.

He let it fly and overthrew her.

She cackled. "You suck, Howl. D-1 my ass."

"Hey now! I'm rusty. Give me another chance."

She scooped up the ball, tucked it under her arm, and ran back to him. "Okay. Here's the deal." She yanked her shirt from her pants and rolled her shoulders like she was getting down to serious business. "Third and long. Two minutes left in the game. We're down by ten. Touchdown and field goal to tie."

"Does the game have playoff implications?"

"Every game has playoff implications." She grinned. "What are you calling?"

"Red Right 22 Texas."

She made a face. "I'm not a running back. Call something for me."

"Just run a deep out route."

He called "hut" twice, and she bolted off the line of scrimmage, running straight ahead for about fifteen yards, and then turned out. By then, his pass was zipping toward her. When it hit her arms, she whooped, and then she kept on running to the tree line.

"Touchdown!" she yelled.

"I think you stepped out of bounds back here." His face hurt from smiling.

"You're full of shit!" She ran back to him, and by the time she stood in front of him, she was winded. "That was a perfect route," she said between breaths.

"I don't know, Bell. I still think you crossed the line."

"It wouldn't be the first time." Her eyes sparkled, and his gut clenched.

He had the urge to kiss her again. But that would definitely be crossing a line. He dropped his gaze to her lips. Nobody was watching here. There was no reason to perpetuate the ruse.

"Why did you agree to come here with me?" she asked softly.

He blinked, shook off the haze, and smiled. "I didn't agree. You led me here."

"No, I mean to Charity in the first place. You said it will give you leverage on the field, but..." she pulled her bottom lip between her teeth, "threatening to bench me would give you leverage, too. I think there's something else. I mean why would a guy like you want to help a girl like me fix a mess I clearly made on my own?"

Man, it was a loaded question. He looked at the football tucked in the crook of her arm and then reached for it, his fingers brushing her skin. She released it to him, and he cradled it with both hands. "I know a little something about making messes and having to clean them up on your own. It's not easy. When I enlisted, I was already a scholarship athlete with all roads pointing to the NFL. I was my father's greatest Pop Warner success story, but I became his biggest disappointment when I joined the Marines. And I made it worse by not talking to him first." He whistled. "It got ugly. There was a lot of yelling. He said a lot of things that I resented."

Carter squeezed the ball as the memories flooded in. "My father said I was a coward and that I was afraid I wasn't good enough to play in the NFL. He said my mother wouldn't have been happy. In fact, she would've been ashamed of me for quitting. It tore me apart; it tore the family apart. By the time I left, he and I were no longer speaking." He loosened his grip on the ball, watching his knuckles return to a healthy shade of pink. "My sister and brother and I were on better terms, but things were still so tense. I slept at Amanda's house the night before I left for basic, and

I remember walking into my niece's room in the middle of the night and breaking down because I thought I'd ruined my family."

Jillian stared at him, wide-eyed and a little belligerent. "That sucks," was all she said.

For some crazy reason, the simple, clear-cut comment made him smile. He dropped the ball and reached for her, pulling her against his chest. "Yeah, it did suck, but it got better—a lot better. And things are going to get better for you and your family, too." He smoothed a hand over her back, along her shoulder, and then slipped it beneath her hair until he had a gentle hold on her neck. "That's why I'm here. I want to help you because I've been there, done that."

She tilted her head back to look up at him. "You know, this might just be the pity talking, but I think I'm starting to like you better than Coach Malloy."

"Oh you think, huh?" He squeezed the back of her neck until she was buckled over, squirming with laughter.

That's when he felt it again. An undeniable spark. And even though two tours of duty in Iraq proved his dad had been wrong— that he was no coward—Carter was scared to death. Jillian Bell was not his type. From everything he'd seen and still more that she'd told him, her brand of chaos would obliterate his orderly world.

But as he chased her around that field, he suddenly wondered if that would be so bad.

Chapter Ten

Jillian crawled out of bed and held her breath as she opened the door of her childhood bedroom. It didn't squeak like it used to when she'd been a teenager trying to sneak out, but her parents' bedroom door was open as an extra deterrent. The glow of the moon from their bedroom window spilled into the hallway, and she could see the closed door to Wendy's old room where Carter now slept. Jillian smiled. Her parents had given him that room on purpose, so Jillian would have to get past them to get to him—squeaky floorboards and all.

They sorely underestimated her powers of stealth movement.

Her heart rate kicked up. Feeling that rush was almost enough to make her abandon her original plan and head in Carter's direction instead, but she looked at the door at the other end of the hall, and something else had a greater pull on her heart.

She tiptoed down the hallway and stood on the landing where the back staircase split. One set of steps led down to the kitchen, the other set led up to the attic bedrooms. She stared into the darkness, listening for any sounds. If Bob caught her, he'd probably make a big deal out of her sneaking around. She looked down where the light above the kitchen sink cast a soft glow on the bottom steps. She could always go raid the Oreos. But then she thought about the things Carter had said earlier, and these thoughts carried her quietly up the steps until she stood in the middle of her nephew's bedroom looking into the crib.

A ceramic turtle nightlight glowed bright enough that she could see Caleb's face as he slept. Chubby cheeks, miniature lips, and the tiniest fist she'd ever seen nestled against his neck. Her heart rate settled, and a fuzzy feeling clogged her chest.

She moved closer, studied him more intently, and held her own breath so she could listen to him breathe. He was perfect. Except, according to doctors, he wasn't. How did they even perform surgery on something so small? That was probably a big part of the risk. God, if anything happened to him …

Now more than ever, she understood how important it was for her to be a part of this family.

"You're going to be just fine, buddy. I'm going to be here for you and your mama whenever you need me." And Caleb would need her, because somebody had to teach him that there was life outside Charity.

"Hey."

She jumped, spun around, and saw Wendy wrapped in a robe, standing in the doorway. "Oh, hey. I … couldn't sleep."

Wendy smiled as she settled into the rocking chair just inside the door. "And you came here?"

"I didn't really get a good look at him earlier." She peered into the crib again, and he made the sweetest squeal-like sound that didn't match the sour look on his face. "Bob's damn stopwatch was in the way. Wen, that can't be good."

Wendy made a face. "It's not as bad as it seems. Honestly. Schedules aside, I want to make sure he's eating enough. The heart issues make him sleepy when he's nursing. I'd like to bring him to bed with me so he can graze all night long, but Bob and the pediatrician say that's dangerous."

Timing the feedings to make sure Caleb was getting enough definitely sounded more reasonable than what she'd heard earlier. But still … she wouldn't listen to Bob if he were the last man on earth.

"Would you bring him to me?" Wendy asked.

Jillian looked from her squirming nephew to her sister. "You want *me* to pick him up and carry him all the way over to you."

"Jillie, you can carry a football for how many yards? Surely you can carry a baby 3 feet. Just watch his head."

She looked at his head and then thought about his heart. Did she have to be careful of that, too? "Oh God. Okay." She could do this. After everything, Wendy trusted her with Caleb. That was big. Jillian wasn't going to mess this up. "Here goes."

She slipped a hand beneath his neck and one beneath his bottom and raised him a few inches off the mattress. He was a lot heavier than he looked, and he didn't like being held like this. His squeal became a cry. *Now what?* On instinct, she leaned over the railing and brought him closer to her chest. His open mouth dragged across her collarbone. "You're a hungry bug."

"Always," Wendy said. Her arms were open, and there was a dreamy look in her eyes. So much joy.

Motherhood had never been high on Jillian's list of must-try things. It seemed unrealistic that she would be happy tethered to a needy little something who cramped her style night and day, but as he snuggled his sweet little face into her neck, a shiver of something wonderful blanketed her skin. Someday, she definitely wanted this.

She passed the baby off to her sister and then sat cross-legged on the floor at her feet. "What about the stopwatch?" she asked, only half teasing.

Wendy set the chair rocking as the baby nursed. "I don't use it for the nighttime feedings." She gestured with her head toward the daybed across the room. "In fact, I usually lay with him over there. What Bob doesn't know won't hurt him."

Jillian liked the sound of that. "So Bob sleeps while you take care of his baby?"

"Bob takes care of the farm, and I take care of our baby. Believe me, I have the better gig."

Maybe. "Do you ever get a night off?"

"I don't want a night off."

Jillian made a face.

"Okay, fine. I do dream of sleeping through the night again, but Mom says once you become a mother, you never sleep through the night again. Too much worry."

"Especially if the kid's like me," Jillian said jokingly, but then a knowing quiet settled over the room.

"Or if he has a heart condition," Wendy said. "But we're optimistic a couple surgeries max will be all it takes to repair the valve. Lord knows enough people are praying for him already."

Jillian nodded. God would help Wendy and Caleb. After all, she was a "good girl."

"You know what else Mom says? That someday you're going to have a little one just like you—she's praying for that, too."

Ha! Wouldn't that be karma at its finest? Jillian untwisted her legs and pulled her knees to her chest. "I don't know about that. I'm not exactly on the motherhood track."

"You never know." Wendy smiled. "You're still young, and now you have Carter."

Jillian blinked up at her sister, then dropped her chin to her knee. *Tell her. Come clean. Let her know it might sound crazy but you did it for her ... and Caleb.*

"He seems like a really great guy," Wendy said.

"He is."

"And he's cute! He looks like Superman or something."

Like Thor, Jillian thought. An image of his gorgeous face and infectious smile floated in her mind. "He's not bad," she said grinning.

"Do you love him?"

She straightened. "Of course not."

"You don't think you could ever love him?"

In a perfect world. Better yet, in a fictional world. Neither of which existed outside this weird weekend she'd created. "Wendy, I ... Carter and I ... I'm ..."

"Confused. I get it. But whatever is going on between you, it sure looks wonderful. I wasn't going to tell you this, but I saw you two in the yard. I, uh, saw Carter kiss you."

"*You* were spying on me." Jillian would've put money on the peeping Tom being a peeping Bob.

"I didn't mean to. I was coming out to apologize for not telling you that Reverend Winters would be here, but then I saw you two together, and you were laughing and talking and looking so cute I didn't want to interrupt. Then he grabbed you and kissed you." The rocking chair squeaked as Wendy lifted Caleb onto her shoulder and patted his back. "I stood there, frozen, thinking Bob has never kissed me like that."

Dang. Jillian dropped her chin to her knees and stared at her sister amid a wave of sadness. Wendy deserved better. She'd been the good girl all these years, and Bob was her reward?

Being the bad girl definitely had perks.

"Are you mad I spied on you?" Wendy asked.

"No," Jillian said.

"Good. Then tell me what it's like. What does it feel like to be kissed like that?"

"It's ..." her voice faded away on the memory of Carter's strong arms around her waist and the taste of him on her lips, "nice."

"Oh, come on. Nice was when Bob kissed me on the forehead after I'd given birth. Nice is when Dad kisses Mom on the cheek when he comes in from the fields. Carter open-mouth kissed you in broad daylight, like a cable movie. That has to be more than nice."

Jillian suppressed a laugh at her sister's naivety. Truth be told, the kiss had been way more than nice ... until Carter called it what it was—nothing more than something that would lend legitimacy to their charade. Before that, it had felt like everything she never knew she wanted, followed by an overwhelming feeling that she never wanted it to end.

"It's hard to explain," she said, knowing full well she didn't have the guts to come clean to Wendy.

"Are you sleeping with him?"

"No!" And true as it was, with her track record, she doubted anyone in Charity would believe her. Which suddenly seemed like such a shame. Ironic really, that this time, she wanted credit for being a good girl.

"I'm sorry I'm being so nosey. I'm just starved for juicy conversation." She settled Caleb at her other breast. "I miss you so much."

Jillian wrapped a hand around her little sister's ankle and squeezed. "I miss you, too."

That settled it. She was going to throw herself into the rest of this weekend and be the best sister she could be. With Carter by her side, she would pull it off like a champ. And maybe, just maybe—*Oh, girl, come on! You know you mean probably*—she would convince him to lay those fabulous lips on her again. In the spirit of legitimacy.

• • •

Carter stared at the ceiling and listened to the rooster crow. He didn't need the wakeup call, he'd been up for about an hour now, tossing and turning, telling himself that among other things, this weekend was about living outside his usual schedule. But damn it! No matter what he told himself, he couldn't fall back asleep, which left him two options: get up and go through his usual routine in a strange house or stare at the ceiling.

He got up, made the twin bed with the creaky brass headboard, and pulled on his running clothes. After a quick stop in the bathroom down the hall, he crept downstairs and out the backdoor. The crisp May air stole his breath, so he started slowly, jogging along the dirt road that led away from the house. Without streetlights, he couldn't see much more than early morning shadows. Not a comforting thought, considering the ruts that nearly swallowed his car. But as the sun rose, he found a smooth path in the road and quickened his pace. He glanced at his watch and decided to run thirty minutes out, then thirty minutes back, which should give the rest of the house time to get up and moving. He pressed the button to set the stopwatch and thought better of it. He would free run today. And hopefully when he got back, Jillian would be awake. He didn't want to be creeping around without her. She knew the ins and outs of the place and the people. She also made everything more fun.

His stomach twisted the smallest bit. Bob or no Bob, he shouldn't have kissed her. Now he couldn't forget the way she felt … the way she tasted. It was like a carb overload that would bite him in the ass and have him begging to sleep it off later. Not good. Not good at all. He couldn't afford to get confused on this mission. Yes, they needed to be convincing, but they didn't need to be *that* convincing. He simply wouldn't go there again. Easy. His stomach twisted harder.

He should've eaten.

When he finally made it back to the house, the front door was open, and he could see the outlines of people through the screen. Two women. One was holding the baby. He slowed his pace as he reached the porch and leaned into a stretch with his leg propped on a step.

The screen door opened, and he looked up to find Jillian wrapped in a bathrobe, smiling brightly at him, with a baby comfortably cradled in her arms.

"Good morning," she said.

She looked … He blinked, smiled, and straightened. She looked …

"You're in shock, aren't you?" She chuckled. "Me, too. But I could totally do this motherhood thing." She winked at him. "I never realized holding a baby isn't much different from holding a football. You do it reverently and carefully, right?" She kissed the sleeping baby's head, but kept her sparkling eyes on Carter. "How was your run?"

He nodded. *Speak, idiot.* "Good."

She chuckled again. "Blueberry muffins are on the counter. They're fresh."

And full of way more carbs than he needed.

She turned around and walked back into the house, leaving him staring at the space where she'd been. She'd looked so ... beautiful. Warm and soft. And he thought about how much better his morning would be if he could go to her and place a kiss on those glorious lips. Maybe he would. He'd wait until she put the baby down and back her into a dark corner of the house and ...

"Morning," said a man's voice from behind him.

Thoroughly flustered, Carter turned to find Mr. Bell dressed in dirty jeans, a flannel shirt, and a baseball cap. "Morning, sir."

"An early riser, huh? I can appreciate that."

Carter nearly choked on the irony and tugged his shirt over his dick. "Yes, sir. Out for a run."

"You have time for a quick walk?"

Under the circumstances he and Jillian had created, this was not a request he could say no to—no matter how badly he wanted to decline and escape. "Of course."

"Good. I have one more trough to fill, and I could use some company."

Carter had a feeling there was more to it than that. Once they cleared the house and had the barn in their sights, he got his confirmation.

"My oldest daughter is what they call a nonconformist," Mr. Bell said. "I imagine you already know this what with those tattoos and some of the things that come out of her mouth. And yet, she walked into my home yesterday looking and acting like someone else—for the most part. A man can't be greedy." He chuckled. It was much deeper than Jillian's laugh, but it had the same staccato sound. Funny how genetics linked people together by the strangest things. "I'm pretty sure I owe this transformation to you."

No. The clothes. The hair. All her. Because she wanted to get it right where Wendy was concerned. Her father needed to know the lengths she was willing to go to be a part of this family, but Carter didn't feel at liberty to point-blank tell him. "Wendy and Caleb mean a lot to her. She just..." *Careful, Carter.* Knowing someone for two weeks—playing a couple for a couple days— hardly qualified him to speak on her behalf, "wants to be a part of the family." So much for being a nonconformist.

Mr. Bell nodded and grabbed a bucket off a fence post. "And we want her to be a part it. We're also happy to have you as a part of it ..."

Oh, man. This was getting carried away. "Mr. Bell..."

"I cleaned the..." Bob's words stopped abruptly when he saw Carter and Mr. Bell.

Mr. Bell held up a hand keeping Bob silenced. "Go ahead, son," he said to Carter, and Bob's eyes narrowed. "You were about to ask me something."

No, he wasn't. He'd been close to coming clean—sort of—if only he could find a way to do it without it coming back to hurt Jillian. But he wasn't about to give up anything in front of Bob. So Carter faced Jillian's father, who waited to be asked some mystery question that came on the heels of him professing his happiness at Carter being a part of the family. *Shit.* Carter could only think of one question that would fit the bill. How was he going to talk himself out of this one?

"Hey!"

All three men looked toward the voice.

Jillian was charging toward them. She was dressed for the christening. A red sweater whipped open over a white, floral-printed sundress that plastered to her shapely thighs. She had the fiercest look on her face, and he knew … he was about to be rescued.

Relief flooded his body.

"This man needs to shower right now." She grabbed his arm and pulled him back toward the house. "We're on a tight schedule this morning. Geez!"

She booked them out of ear- and eyeshot. When they were a few feet from the back door, she asked, "Are there any fires I need to put out back there?"

"Nope. But had you taken any longer, I might have been cornered into asking your dad for your hand."

She stopped and looked at him. "No shit? You were willing to take it that far?"

He nodded. "I guess so."

"I'm not sure what that says about you, Carter Howl."

"It says I'm the kind of guy you can depend on whatever the mission."

She smiled. "Maybe. It also says underneath all that composure, you're as crazy as I am." She laughed. "I love it! See, I told you I'd be teaching you some things this weekend. Glad to see you're a fast learner." She lifted onto her toes and kissed him. Simple. Sweet. And still, lust shot through him. "For legitimacy's sake," she whispered as she dropped back to her normal height. But there was nothing legitimate about the way she was eyeing him up and licking her lips. "You know? We could probably use more practice." She kissed him again. Hotter now. Tip of her tongue tangling with his. Hands crawling up his stomach to his chest. Fingernails gently scraping the base of his neck.

Fuck it. He wrapped her up in his arms and opened wide. Why squander a limited opportunity?

"Much better," Jillian said, when they finally took a breath.

He couldn't argue with that.

Chapter Eleven

After the baptism, a crowd converged on Jillian's parents' house. These people loved potluck brunches the way Jillian loved no-cover after hours. She scooted closer to Carter on the couch, making room for more guests. A lot of people didn't seem to recognize her. That, or they thought of her like the plague and stayed the hell away. That was how she was thinking of Bob and Keller. Having Carter here made avoiding them that much easier.

She slipped a hand between his hard body and his strong arm and hooked him. For legitimacy's sake. She'd done it enough at the church that it felt natural now. And they stayed that way while he talked to Skip David, Charity's one-stop insurance salesman and her parents' nearest neighbor, about the success of Shock & Awe.

"And then you two met playing football?" Skip asked.

"Yep," Carter said, and to her surprise, his palm landed softly, easily on her thigh. "But she plays. I coach."

"Ain't there a conflict of interest there?" Skip laughed.

She felt Carter's hand tighten the tiniest bit around her leg. "Nope. We know how to keep things separate," she said.

"At least she's not calling the shots, huh?" Skip asked. "That would be a little harder to swallow."

This time, it was her arm tightening around Carter's as she felt the fake smile fall off her face. Would it be bad form to call Skip David a misogynistic asshole on the heels of a church service?

"I'd let her call the shots anytime," Carter said. He smoothed his hand up and down her thigh just enough to diffuse the anger. "She's smart, and she's tough, and she has more talent than men twice her size. Gender has nothing to do with it."

Happy sigh. "What he said." She looked up at him and didn't care one bit if it looked as dreamy as it felt. But then she remembered he was playing a part. *Chameleons survive in the desert.* Wasn't that what he'd said? Maybe that was all this was. She'd witnessed enough of his rule-oriented behavior to know it had to still be there underneath this open-minded, flexible demeanor. *Don't get sucked in*, said the voice in her head. *Tomorrow you'll be right back to running laps.*

"Excuse me," she said. Now would be a good time to hop off the crazy train and take a few quiet minutes to herself in the bathroom. "I'll be right back."

She passed through the kitchen and smiled at her mother, who was looking better today. Her mother smiled back, but there was still a hesitation, like the woman couldn't completely let down her guard while Jillian was here. It made Jillian want to get to the bathroom faster.

She turned into the hall and saw that the door was closed to the bathroom tucked beneath the backstairs. Even better. Now she had an excuse to go upstairs and leave the party altogether. How long could she hide out?

Before she could reach the first step, she heard a *click-clack* behind her, followed by Keller's voice. "Were you waiting for this?" he asked politely. He swept his hand toward the empty bathroom and smiled, but it looked fake somehow. She hesitated.

"You clean up well, Jillie. It must feel good—to be on the right side finally."

She opened her mouth to counterattack, but Wendy's laughter filtered down the hall from the other room, and like a bad dream, Jillian couldn't force anything out.

He took a couple steps toward her, and she stood tall.

"But I can't help but think of the wolf in sheep's clothing." He smiled again. "It makes me wonder how long it will take your fine and upstanding young man to realize there's nothing fine and upstanding about you. Of course, I could be wrong, but I'm not usually."

His nasty wink broke through her stupor, and she charged him, backing him against the wall. "I don't know how anybody takes spiritual direction from you. You're disgusting. And if the right side is your side, then I'm happy to be wrong."

"Spoken like a true sinner."

"Reverend Winters ..." Her mother's voice was the only thing that kept her from putting him through the wall. "There you are. Sweet Anne is looking for you." She sounded pleasant enough, but there was something steely in her eyes, and that something was no doubt directed at Jillian.

"Thank you, Mrs. Bell." He straightened his tie and shot one last patronizing smile at Jillian. "I wouldn't want to keep my lovely wife waiting."

Gag! Jillian didn't wait for her mother's reprimand. She scurried into the bathroom and locked the door. She was shaking. A few more seconds and she would've assaulted him, which would've brought Officer "Crumb Cake" to the house to most everyone's delight.

She turned on the water full blast, flushed the toilet, and screamed into the crook of her arm. Had her mother heard how awful Keller had been? Did that even matter? Or was he allowed to talk like that because he was a man? If he'd physically hurt her, would that have been okay, too? Because she had it coming behaving like that? She flushed the toilet and screamed again.

Eventually, she killed the water and took a seat on the closed toilet. She stayed there, until someone knocked.

"Just a minute," she called.

After a big inhale and exhale, she focused on the fact that Carter was waiting for her, and she opened the door.

Bob's mother stood against the wall. The minute Betty Novick saw Jillian, her smile faded.

Jillian walked away to the sound of the closing door. She bet Betty lined the toilet seat. The image of the woman spreading tissue out to avoid catching whatever she assumed Jillian had made her finally laugh. This place ... These people ... She was done feeling sorry for herself. It was so much better feeling sorry for them.

As she passed through the kitchen, she noticed her mother leaning against the counter, breathing deeply. Whatever anger and disappointment Jillian had felt toward her withered slightly when faced with her pain.

There had to be some kind of medicine her mother could take. When was the last time she'd seen a rheumatologist? They needed to talk about something other than this baptism.

Jillian cut between the farmhouse table and the hutch on her way to her mother, but someone grabbed her wrist.

"Jillie?"

She turned toward the familiar voice and saw Bruce, Bob's brother, smiling at her.

She'd been able to avoid him at the church, but she knew she wouldn't be so lucky if he showed up here.

He tugged on her arm, pulling her into a hug that had people staring. *Ooh, look! The wedding crashers are at it again.*

She started to push away.

"I barely recognized you!" He let her go and roughly pushed up her sleeve. "Woo!" He wiped the back of his hand over his forehead. "Thank God. I thought maybe you erased everything I love about you. I should've known better. Just playing the game right?" He winked. His eyes were glassy. She didn't smell a hint of alcohol, so that glassy stare could only mean one other thing. Drugs. She bit into her bottom lip. The last two years had not been kind to him.

Across the room, Bob moved the slightest bit closer, and he was glaring at her. She swallowed the anger that mixed with concern for Bruce. "It's good to see you again," she said cautiously.

He made a face and tightened his grip. "What's wrong with you, Jillie? You medicated?" He laughed. "Come on. Let's get out of here."

She was about to pull her arm away when she heard, "Hey, man. Carter Howl. I don't believe we've met." Carter's huge body forced its way into the gap between the wall and the table and pressed against her back. His strong hand reached between them in introduction and challenge to Bruce.

"I'm sorry, babe." The words sort of tumbled out as she glanced up at him. "I should've introduced you at the church, but we got sidetracked."

Carter's jaw was set, and his eyes were dark as he looked back and forth between Bruce's hand, which was still wound tightly around her arm, and Bruce's snarling face.

Babe? Her tongue felt tacky. That happened way too easily. "This is Bob's brother, Bruce. Bruce, this is my boyfriend, Carter."

Bruce let go.

"Honey, come on." Betty swooped in with a smile for her son and a scowl for Jillian. "I'll make a plate for you, so you can eat. There's Rice Krispies treats—your favorite."

Oh, that was rich. By all means, coddle your adult son who is clearly under the influence of something and get him out of that awful Jillian's clutches before she influences him badly again.

When Betty and Bruce walked away, Jillian shot Bob a look that said, "Your family is fucked up." But he simply smiled back as if to say, "Bravo, Jillie!" *Asshole.* She looked around at everyone else who was staring at her. A lot of self-righteous smiles filled the room. Except for Keller and Anne, who were huddled in a corner looking like they pitied her.

It was wedding reception 2.0. Only this time, Jillian hadn't done anything wrong.

"He's high!" she said loudly. "I'm sober. Sadly and completely sober, so why is everyone looking at me like I'm the problem here?"

Carter's hand was on her back, and she knew he was willing her to calm down, but she'd had enough of it. All of it. "Whatever." She pushed through the crowd and headed for the door. That was when she saw Wendy's wide, wet eyes.

Great. Whether she'd meant to or not, Jillian had screwed up again.

•••

"Why can't I keep my mouth shut?"

Jillian was sitting on a stump several hundred yards away from the house, on the far side of the barn, behind a derelict shed that hid her from the world. It had taken Carter ten whole minutes to find her, because she wouldn't answer his texts or calls.

When he reached her, he squatted down in front of her, not surprised to see more anger than sadness on her face.

"One fucking weekend was all I needed to get through, and I couldn't do it." She lifted her chin and rolled her eyes. "I shouldn't have come. We shouldn't have come. It would've been better for me to make the trip some other time by myself." She shook her head. "They all think I'm the same old Jillian."

He hated hearing her talk like that. What he'd seen over the past twenty-four hours was a fun-loving woman who was miserably misunderstood. With a finger beneath her chin, he turned her head so he could look at her good and hard. "There's nothing wrong with the same old Jillian."

"Ha! This coming from the man who wanted to muzzle me that first practice."

He hated hearing that, too. Abrasive though she'd been, he'd never thought for a minute about doing anything other than getting through to her. "Give me some credit," he said. "I wouldn't even muzzle a dog."

"Fine, but you sure looked like you wanted me to shut up. Like they all wanted me to shut up in there."

"Nope. It's different, especially now that I know you." He dropped his hand to her neck and smoothed a thumb across her cheek. "You're an incredibly talented football player, a passionate friend and teammate, a kick-ass band promoter."

"Go on." She grinned. "I'm definitely starting to feel better."

"You're free spirited, strong willed, and beautiful."

Her lips parted the slightest bit.

"And I like the unpredictability of being with you."

"Liar," she said, but she was laughing. "Thank you. You made me feel much better. You're good at that. Actually, you're good at a lot of things. Kissing probably tops the list." The faintest dusting of red brightened her cheeks. "You're also a good listener. You give good advice, and I can honestly say you've become a good friend." She reached up and wrapped a hand around his wrist.

He wasn't feeling very friendly right now. Whatever was happening here was going to cause one hell of a mess at home, but ... the longer he looked at her, the more he knew that he didn't want whatever was between them to end. Not yet. Not until it had run its course.

Leaning in, he brushed his lips over hers. Back and forth, a gentle tease. But then a swell of emotion carried both of his hands to her face, and he coaxed her mouth open with his tongue, angling his head to deepen the kiss. She curled her fingers into his dress shirt, and the kiss deepened still. Long and slow until the world around them drifted away.

"For legitimacy's sake," she said when they finally came up for air, but there was a question in her beautiful brown eyes.

Carter licked the taste of her from his lips and shook his head. "For my sake. Because I wanted to."

Her wistful smile faded on the next breeze. "Now what?"

"I'm not sure."

"We should leave." She laced her fingers with his and stood.

Oh. He'd been talking about them, as in he wasn't sure what happened now between them. But she'd been talking about Charity.

He straightened. "I get why you want to leave, I do, but letting them chase you off sends the wrong message." He squeezed her hand. "If your buttons can be pushed, then people are going to push them."

She seemed to think about it as she tipped her head to the sky and watched a flock of noisy birds pass overhead. Then she exhaled loudly and let go of his hand. "It would be so much easier to just leave."

Like he'd "just" enlisted. "Easy isn't always better. Trust me. You leave stuff behind when you go—unfinished business—and it just waits there for you to come back. At some point, you have to deal with it. You have to confront the issue. You have to stop running from it."

"Is that what you did with your family when you ran off and joined the Marines—confronted the issue?"

He didn't want to analyze his actions. He wanted to temper hers. "Let's just say eventually I had to take a good, hard look at the situation and accept the part I played in it. Then I had to apologize for that. It definitely wasn't easy, because I wasn't 100 percent convinced I'd done anything wrong. But I realized I wanted to be a part of my family more than I wanted to be right."

She looked a little green around the gills. "I'm not going in there and apologizing for anything while half the town is gawking."

"I wouldn't expect you to," Carter said. "We can wait until the rest of them leave."

"But what if it's late? We have to get back. You have to work early tomorrow."

He shrugged. "I own the company. Surely I can go in late if I want to. Nobody's going to yell at me."

She grinned.

"Then that settles it." He turned toward the house and gently pulled her along behind.

"Are you sure about this?"

He glanced back. "Absolutely." He was pretty sure about her, too.

He'd found his spark. Now, he just needed to find a way to keep it burning when they got back to Cleveland.

• • •

Jillian's phone read

7:10 PM

By the time the last guests left. Somehow she'd managed to make it through four additional hours of small talk and frustrating innuendos about her behavior. Carter had kept her pretty well shielded, though. And Wendy ... she'd been so surprised and happy to see Jillian return that neither she nor Caleb left her side for anything more than diaper changes and feedings.

But now, she had to do what she'd stayed to do. She had to confront the issue head on. And maybe even apologize. *Ugh*. Easier said than done.

"I'm going to change and milk the cows," Bob said.

Jillian's father looked from Bob to her and Carter. "I'll join you shortly. Let me say my goodbyes first."

Wendy sat with the baby at the kitchen table, while their mother piled dirty dishes on the counter beside the sink.

What a ridiculous scene of gender imbalance. "I'm not going anywhere," Jillian said. "Carter and I will clean up first. Mom, you need to go lay down." A confrontation could wait.

Her mother glanced up and, for a split second, looked relieved.

"Nonsense. You two have a long ride home. We can manage."

"No," Jillian said. And the tone of her voice attracted everyone's attention, even Bob's. "That's ridiculous. You can't be expected to clean up this entire mess alone."

"Wendy is here," Bob said.

"Wendy is taking care of your baby," Jillian snapped. "What is wrong with you?"

To her surprise, Carter didn't try to stop her impending tirade, he simply brushed past her and guided her mother away from the sink. "I insist," he said. "My sister would insist. I help her clean the kitchen every Sunday."

Bob scoffed at Carter's chivalry and then focused his ire on Jillian. "Happy you messed up another event?"

"I didn't mess up anything. Bruce is to blame for that."

"I refuse to listen to this." Bob stormed up the stairs.

"Jillie," Wendy whispered, looking scared to death. "What are you doing?"

"Believe it or not, trying to make things better."

Carter gave her an encouraging glance. It helped when she registered the looks of horror and disappointment on her parents' faces. His words from earlier that day helped, too. *Accept the part I played in it, and then apologize for that.*

She took a big breath. "I've made mistakes. We can all agree on that. I'm sorry I screwed up at Wendy's wedding. I'm sorry I ran out of here a couple times this weekend. I'm sorry I had words with Keller in the hallway instead of walking away. But there's always going to be a part of me that calls a spade a spade when I see it." She shoved up the sleeves of her sweater. "I am who I am." Nobody made an ounce of eye contact with her. "Will you ever be able to love me, or did I actually give up any chance of that when I refused to become Keller's cookie-cutter wife?"

"I love you," Wendy said, a tear streaming down her cheek.

And in the midst of the intense scene, Jillian smiled. "I know you do." But then she turned to her parents, who looked unmoved.

"Of course, we love you," her father said in a monotone voice that did nothing to convince her.

Wrinkles lined her mother's face. "Love is a two-way street. At either end is sacrifice and compromise. You don't know what those words mean."

Jillian balked. "Of course I do! Why do you think I'm here? Why do you think I dragged him here?" This was all so stupid, and in the end, the charade didn't matter one bit. She was still going to roll out of town as the hated woman. Well, then so be it. "These aren't even my clothes, and..." she looked at Carter, a brief apology for wasting his time in her eyes, "he's not even my boyfriend."

"I knew it!" Of course, Bob had managed to make it back in time for that. "Your Facebook status says you're single! There's not a mention of the guy on there."

Ooh! Good catch. She should have thought of that.

"Because I'm her fiancé."

Jillian rolled her eyes at Carter's ludicrous statement.

"Young man, you never asked for her hand!" her father said.

"Where's the ring?" Bob asked.

Jillian shook her head. "There is no ring, because..."

"I haven't officially asked her yet. I wanted to ask for her hand first, sir, but I chickened out." Carter dropped to one knee like some cheesy prince in a fairy-tale movie.

"Oh my God!" Jillian said. "Get up." She tugged on his hand, but he knelt his ground.

"Oh my goodness," her mother corrected, but the woman was on the edge of her seat.

Jillian rolled her eyes again, exasperated at the bizarre turn of events.

"Say yes," Wendy said. "It's the sweetest thing I've ever seen."

"It's not for real," Bob said.

"Say yes." This time, the words came from Carter, who was looking up at her like a deer in headlights. "Then we can ride off into the sunset." She knew he was either desperately trying to one-up Bob or salvage the mission. Probably both. And as outrageous as it was, the fact that he would go this far for her ... She pressed a hand over her pounding heart. Had anyone ever gone that far for her?

Oh, why not? Might as well give Wendy a little excitement and end this thing with a bang.

Jillian laughed. "Fine. Yes."

Bob groaned, but no one else seemed to object.

Someday soon, she'd have to burst their little bubble, tell them all she and Carter weren't engaged. Maybe she'd have a little fun with it and tell them Carter had admitted he was gay.

The next thing she knew, Carter scooped her up and planted a completely Charity-inappropriate kiss on her lips.

Yeah, nobody would believe that. She was going to have to come up with something else.

Chapter Twelve

Carter hooked Jillian's arm around his and led her out of the farm-house on the heels of their goodbyes. This was it, the end of the charade. And time for him to seriously consider his next move.

He didn't want this to end, which was partially the reason why he'd lost his mind back there, trying to hold everything together. The other part just wanted to knock that smug look off Bob's face. As Jillian folded into his car and he closed the door, he knew having a personal relationship with her wouldn't be easy. They butted heads at every turn, and he was her coach for God's sake. What would his father say?

"You're an idiot," she said, when he closed himself inside the car and pulled away from the farmhouse. "Remind me to never let you lead a mission again."

Yep, forever butting heads. But she was smiling.

"Why would you do something like that?" she asked.

"Somebody had to do something. I wasn't going to let you go and waste all that progress."

"You think I made progress?"

"Yes." He reached across the console and grabbed her hand. "I think *we* made progress, and I'd like to keep going that way."

She puzzled at him.

"We're good together, Jillian."

She laughed and wiggled her hand free. "You're crazy. It would never work. You're not my type."

"I seemed like your type when you were kissing me."

She stayed quiet a beat too long, and then she rushed in with, "Because I was playing a part. You were playing a part."

Maybe, but not all of it was fake. You couldn't fake feelings like that. "Underneath it all, I was me, and you were you."

She dropped her head to the seatback and stared out the windshield. "I don't date nice guys," she said.

"Why's that?"

She pushed her sleeve up and pointed at that damn tattoo. "They never live up to expectations."

He scoffed. "Keller is not a nice guy."

"He was when he was getting his way. The minute I started wanting things my way, he flipped. You're sort of like that, too," she said with a saucy grin.

Carter growled under his breath at the connection. "I'm nothing like that man."

"You're a lot better looking, that's for sure."

"Okay fine. Let's go with that. What if you use me for my looks?"

She laughed. "I'd rather use you for your body?"

"Whatever works. Because I'm serious. I think there's something here." He waved a hand back and forth between them.

After another exaggerated pause, she said, "I'll think about it."

He brought the car to an abrupt stop on the side of the dirt road and reached for her, pulling her tight against her seatbelt so that her upper body reached his. "Think about this," he said, and then he kissed her soundly, threading his fingers through her hair.

A few sweeps of his tongue. A nibble on her bottom lip. He cupped her neck, skirted her shoulders, and grazed her breasts. "Think about this," he said again.

God knew he would.

•••

Like the freaking three fates, Tanya, Jade, and MJ were waiting for Jillian when she walked through the door.

"How'd it go?" Tanya asked.

She dropped her suitcase by the door and took a deep breath. "It was ... actually, it was good ... for the most part." But it was so nice to be home—really home.

"What part wasn't good?" MJ eyed her up carefully, like she was trying to read a particularly sneaky defense.

"Carter and I are fine if that's what you're getting at. Nothing bad happened there." In fact, she was still reeling from his admission in the car—and that kiss. Yes, she was thinking about that kiss.

She needed a chair.

"How 'bout something good?" Tanya asked, suspiciously.

Jade just sat there, the pickle in the middle of a pair who knew for better or for worse what Jillian was capable of.

"I did not sleep with him." She stood a little straighter despite the voice in her head that added a *yet*. "All we did was kiss."

Three pairs of eyebrows raised skeptically.

"Girl, you never just kiss," Tanya said.

"This time, I did. Trust me. There weren't many opportunities for anything else."

"Thank God," MJ said under her breath.

"Is he a good kisser?" Jade asked.

The other two shot her disapproving looks.

"What? I'm curious," Jade said.

"We don't need to know that," MJ said. "He's our coach. Period."

The memories bombarded Jillian, and she couldn't help herself. "He's a very good kisser."

Jade smiled. "I knew it! He just looks like he knows his way around a kiss."

MJ groaned. "This was a bad idea."

But it hadn't been. "We made progress."

"That's awesome," Jade said.

Tanya smiled and then reached out to pat Jillian's hand. "Good for you."

Except she wasn't really sure if she was talking more about the progress with her family or with Carter.

MJ remained quiet. Probably because her own family was an excruciatingly slow work in progress.

Jillian filled them in on her battles with Keller and Bob. She even told them about the random proposal. Tanya laughed. MJ looked horrified.

"I'm really starting to doubt his judgment," MJ said. "I don't see how you can think it's no big deal. You kissed the man! You two were ..." MJ waved a hand, "carrying on like idiots. How is that not going to impact your relationship on field?"

Jillian sighed. She was tired, and she really wasn't in the mood for a lecture. She'd never had trouble meshing her personal and professional lives before.

"It'll be fine." She squeezed MJ's shoulders as she passed.

And tomorrow night at practice, she would prove it. As far as the team went, nothing had changed.

• • •

Monday evening, Carter took a big breath before he walked through the football stadium gates and faced his father. He still wasn't sure the best way to broach the subject of Charity. Part of him wanted to come clean completely, so he could date Jillian aboveboard. The other part wanted to hold back, because he didn't want to give his father a chance to kill it dead in the water. He didn't want to repeat past mistakes.

"Dad," he said. "How's it going?"

His father looked up from the open playbook on his desk. "It's going well. How 'bout for you? Was the mission a success?"

Carter swallowed the unrest and nodded. "It was good."

His father met him with a blank stare. "Good? That's all I get? I would've thought your recon skills better than that. Do you think she'll settle down now?"

"I do." She already seemed more settled and sensible to him. Then again, maybe he only thought that because he was seeing her in a different light. He rubbed a hand across his forehead and tried to forget his confusion.

"Son?" His father's voice was cautious. "You seem awfully nervous. Something you want to tell me?"

"I like her." It came out in one big breath.

"Come again?"

"I have feelings for Jillian."

His father's eyes flashed angry before he looked down at the desk again. "Well then, unfeel them."

"It doesn't work that way."

"In this office, it works the way I say it works!" His father slammed a hand against the desk. "I will not condone inappropriate relationships between a member of the coaching staff and this team. I saw a sexual harassment lawsuit bring down an entire franchise my first season in the league. These women need to trust us, not feel preyed upon."

"I'm not preying on her!" And the fact that his father thought he was capable of something like that was disgusting. "We're consenting adults."

Again, his hand met the table. "You can't effectively manage someone you're involved with. You lose your leverage, damn it! She already questions your authority. Imagine what she'll do if she thinks you like her too much to make her toe the line. How will you control her then? How will you control any of them if they see you can be tempted? Now, use the head on your shoulders, boy!"

Carter bristled at the insinuation. He'd been thinking long and hard about Jillian, and he knew it wasn't just physical. "Dad, I ..."

"This conversation is over," his father said. "I don't want to hear another foolish word about it. You go out there and show some of that Marine stoicism. On my field, you treat her like she's anybody else. And if you can't, I'll find someone who can. You hear me?"

He wished he hadn't. "I hear you. Loud and clear," he added through clenched teeth.

Carter's dark thoughts hounded him as he took the field. Maybe he should resign. He didn't need this aggravation. But his father would definitely take Carter quitting *this* football team personally. *Arrrgh!* He was so damn tired of worrying about making his father happy.

Jillian jogged onto the field, and Carter froze.

She'd dyed the tips of her hair blue again, and she was laughing. *Treat her like she's anyone else.* From his kicked-up pulse to his shallow breathing, he wasn't sure he was capable of it.

"Reynolds, could you work with the wide receivers today?" he asked. "I want to spend time with the running backs." After all, they'd be getting the bulk of the carries this weekend. And avoiding Jillian seemed like the safest option right now.

But he couldn't avoid her all practice. Eventually, she caught up with him on the sidelines.

"Hey, Coach," she said. There was a twinkle in her eyes and a curve to her lips.

His body reacted immediately, turning on and heating up. But he couldn't get his father's angry words out of his head. "Bell," he said dryly, hoping she would heed his warning.

"Ooh ..." she gave a quick look around them and then lowered her voice suggestively, "that's a bossy tone. I kinda like it."

He ached for her—all of her, but to encourage this would be playing a dangerous game. "Not now," he warned again. Not ever if his father got his way. The anger overshadowed the attraction.

She blinked a few times, looking a little confused. "Is everything okay?"

"Not really."

"Bell!" roared Reynolds. "Since when are you a running back?"

Carter caught sight of his father, who was across the field working with special teams, looking their way. *Damn it!* "Get your ass back over there and join your team."

She made a face. "What is wrong with you?" But she didn't wait for an answer.

He watched her jog into the group of receivers, and then he glanced at his father again. *Happy now?* Because Carter sure as hell wasn't.

Fifteen minutes later, Reynolds called him over to help with one-on-one stalk blocking. Carter glanced at Jillian, and he could tell by the set of her chin that she was pissed at him. Good. It would make it that much easier to treat her like anyone else.

"Show me what you've got," he said to the group.

They were a mess.

As each pair lined up, he offered constructive criticism, positioning their bodies and reminding them of their mission. By the time it was Jillian's turn, he was on autopilot. He grabbed for her hips like he'd done with the four players before her. But she stepped away. Great. They were back to this. "Bell, on the line!"

"I need a water break." She took one step toward the sideline.

"On the line!"

She turned and glared at him, challenge in her eyes.

"Don't push me." His words were low and angry, but he caught the hint of something else in her stare. Desperation?

"Fine," she said. "As long as you don't touch me."

It was so damn quiet he could hear the turf crunching beneath her cleats as she returned to the start position. At some point during the faceoff, the quarterbacks and linewomen had converged on the patch of green behind them. Wide eyes all around. He could only imagine what they were thinking.

Off in the distance, his father observed the drill and offered Carter a quick nod of ... was that approval? It twisted his gut and made him resent the position he'd been put in even more.

He never should've opened his mouth about his feelings for Jillian.

• • •

Jillian sprinted through the parking lot, her pace fueled by anger over the way Carter had treated her and the "I told you so" looks that had been on Tanya's and MJ's faces. No matter what she'd been thinking last night as she drifted off to sleep, Thor's body was not worth the aggravation.

"Bell!"

She picked up her pace, breathing heavy by the time she reached for her car door. It wouldn't open because of Carter's strong hand.

"Listen to me," he said.

She pushed him. "I'm sick of listening to you. You've been barking orders at me all day."

"Because of my dad." He glanced over his shoulder. In the distance, a couple players headed to their cars. "He told me I need to treat you like everyone else."

"You treat me worse than everyone else. So go to hell." She tried the door again.

He leaned against it. "I'll back off."

She didn't believe him. He probably got some sadistic pleasure out of yelling at her.

In the sheltered space between them, he brushed a hand over her hip bone, and she sucked in a shallow breath.

"I swear to you," he said. "It will get easier. I just need to get my father off my back."

His thumb pressed into her flesh, gently, then circled until it stirred up a torrent of unangry things. She released a shaky exhale. Hadn't he just spent a good portion of the weekend helping to keep her parents off her back?

His hand slid the smallest bit higher, and his eyes clouded with heat. She swallowed a wave of lust, and said, "Okay. You go easy on me, and I'll go easy on you."

He smiled as he stared at her lips.

"Unless you want me to make it hard," she said with a grin.

He released a muffled growl. "Not here."

"I didn't think so."

He backed away like he was afraid of what she might do next—in the middle of the stadium parking lot—but he was grinning. "One of these days, Bell. One of these days."

She wasn't sure he had the guts.

Chapter Thirteen

Things between Carter and Jillian did get easier from there. By the end of the week, he'd managed to keep his "bossing" to a minimum. She didn't settle down so much as she capitulated. But every once in a while, she shot him the bird or told him to go to hell. "For legitimacy's sake," she'd said.

He kept trying to figure out a way to get her off the field and into bed. But the week had been a blur with crisis after crisis at work, including a copycat business in Michigan that may or may not be infringing on Shock & Awe's trademark. After hours hadn't been much better. His niece, Sophia, had basketball games on Tuesday and Thursday afternoons. He'd gone straight from work to the middle school and straight from the middle school to the football field. Then straight from the field back to the office until he fell asleep at his desk. He owed the middle-aged couple down the hall a full month's rent for all the hours they'd been taking care of Hercules.

He was so looking forward to a free Friday night until Russ called needing help moving furniture. That's exactly where he was headed when he left the field at 7:00.

He got as far as the gates before he heard a, "Hey!"

He looked back and saw Jillian jogging toward him. Her wet hair left marks on the shoulders of her little pink T-shirt, which read, "Suck It!" right across her breasts. The logo of some hard candy company appeared in smaller script beneath the words, and he shook his head as he laughed.

"What?" she asked.

"Nice shirt."

She grinned. "I like things that have double meanings."

"I know."

They shared a look, and five measly seconds was all it took for him to feel like taking her on the hood of a car.

"My mom wants your address."

"Why?"

"She wants to send an engagement card." She laughed. "Nice mess you got yourself into, huh?"

"You were there, too," he said.

"Yeah, yeah." She waved him off. "I'm going to let her send you the card—for the fun of it—but don't worry, I'm going to break up with you soon."

The breakup wasn't real, because the relationship wasn't real. But real or not, the announcement that she was dumping him felt shitty.

"You're heartless, Bell." He laughed, because he didn't know what else to do.

"You know it." She was fiddling with her phone. "Okay. Hit me."

He rattled off the address, watching her fingers move, listening to her laugh when she screwed up and had to type something over again. He wanted to touch her, thread his fingers through her wet hair, and taste her on his tongue. "Jillian."

She looked up at him, and the laughter faded. Eyes wide, lips parted. Inches away.

"Son! Glad I caught you!"

Carter stepped back and looked beyond her to where his father was standing stone-faced.

"You're heading to Russ's now, right?"

Carter nodded and swiped at the sudden beads of sweat on his forehead.

"See you on the bus tomorrow." Jillian backpedaled away from him. "Look out Detroit!" She fist pumped and then spun around and took off running.

His father regarded him with cool eyes and dropped the pretense now that they were alone. "I thought I made myself clear."

"You did."

"It didn't look that way."

"Dad ..."

"If I see you huddled up with her again, you're ..."

"Gone. Replaced. Written off. I know."

"I don't want it to come to that."

Son of a bitch. Carter exhaled loudly. He was going to have to take control of his libido or risk alienating his dad again.

• • •

At halftime during Saturday's game, Jillian walked into the locker room and let out a scream. "We're running the ball too much." Not a single pass had come her way. "You're going to start calling audibles," she said to MJ. "I want the ball."

"Ladies!" Coach Howl, with Carter by his side, snapped his fingers overhead and spent the next five minutes rattling on about how proud he was with the improvements in the running game.

"We're down fourteen fucking points!" Jillian shouted.

Coach Howl ignored her. Carter, on the other hand, gave her a thinly veiled sympathetic look that made her think maybe he agreed.

After Coach Howl's pep talk wound down, she half expected Carter to approach her, but he didn't. He simply walked out of the locker room behind his father with his tail between his legs. Submission was not sexy unless it involved handcuffs or neckties.

"I'm serious," she said to MJ. "Override something. Get the ball to me. Let's win this thing." Nobody wanted mandatory Sunday films.

Despite the tension that had been brewing between her and MJ ever since Charity, MJ nodded. "If the opportunity arises."

In the third quarter, Jillian caught three passes in a row for a total gain of 67 yards before she hauled in a pass in the end zone to tie the game. "And that's why we're a passing team!" she crowed as she returned to the bench.

Coach Howl sneered at the outburst.

When the fourth quarter saw a return to hard-ass Thor and the precious running game, it was annoying as hell. But when the team marched down the field utilizing nothing but the run and scored a touchdown on third and goal that put them up and on top at the end of the game, she felt like she could take some credit for the win. "Death to Sunday films!" she screamed.

As they boarded the bus for the return trip home, Jillian passed Carter and gave him a wink.

He stiffened. In his defense, his father was nearby, but finally, she'd had enough of it. As fun as it was to tease and tempt him, she was tired of the hot-and-cold game. He was never going to have enough guts to kiss her here like he'd kissed her in Charity.

"Plans tonight?" MJ asked.

Jillian's smile felt too wide. "Of course. Chix are playing at Fall Guys." A little music, a little booze, a little booty. God knew she was long overdue. Carter would be out of her mind by Monday. "Don't wait up," she said to Jade through the crack in the seats. "And don't text me a dozen times worried. I'll be home ... when I get home." Oh, it felt good to be back to normal!

Jade didn't even look up from her book. She just nodded. MJ snuggled against the window to take a call from her husband. And Jillian spent the rest of the drive home staring at the back of Carter's head.

• • •

Like he always did, Carter scrolled through satellite radio stations as he guided the car through the stadium parking lot. The bus had emptied out and pulled away at least fifteen minutes ago while he'd been caught up, rehashing the win with the younger half of the coaching staff. And now, he was headed home for the first quiet night in a week. He still wished he'd be spending it with Jillian.

Like a mirage, she appeared in front of his car, waving her arms again. Her T-shirt rode up her belly as she flagged him down—just like it had the first time. Only this time when he appreciated the smooth curves of her waist and the subtle hips with his eyes, he could remember how they felt in his hands. His throat tightened along with his dick.

"Battery?" he asked through his open window.

"No." She made a face. "This time I don't have keys. I put them in Tanya's purse on the bus ride to Detroit and forgot she was spending the night there with her boyfriend. MJ went to dinner with Tag. I can't get a hold of Jade. I'm stuck ... with you again." Unfortunately, she didn't look too happy about it. "That address you gave me is five minutes from my apartment. Can you give me a ride home?"

He'd like to give her a ride. His body was already prepared to. "Get in the car," he said.

She got in and turned up the radio.

He kept both hands on the wheel, while her hands strummed a beat on her thighs. Every few seconds, he stole a glance at her. With each look, his heart beat harder. Did she have any idea how she tore him up inside? How much he craved more time with her?

He manipulated the controls on the steering wheel to quiet the radio and could've sworn he heard his heart beating. "I was going to stop off for some food on my way home," he said nonchalantly. "Hungry?"

She looked him over. "Uh, actually, I was headed out tonight with friends."

"You couldn't meet up with them later?" He tipped his head toward her and tried to beg with his eyes without losing his dignity. "We haven't had much time to talk. There's a lot to say."

She shrugged. "I don't know about that."

"Come on. I'll buy. You call what and where."

"Angelo's Brick Oven Pizza," she said suddenly. "It's out this way, and it's my favorite. It's also expensive. If you're buying, and I'm hungry, then why not?"

Oh, he could think of a few reasons, the big one being that he was directly defying his father. Still, the swirl of happiness he felt when he was with her made him want this bad enough to believe they wouldn't get caught. "Angelo's it is."

"Wait. What does a carb-phobic guy eat at a pizza place?" She made a face that had him laughing. "A salad?"

"I'm adaptable, remember? I'll eat the pizza, and since it's Saturday night and we won the game, I might even have a beer."

"Maniac," she teased.

He was definitely going to have a beer tonight.

But when they pulled into the lot of Angelo's Brick Oven Pizza, his heart, which had been beating so soundly, stopped. *That* looked like his father's truck. And this was a place his family had been known to frequent. "Shit."

"You don't like to wait?"

"Huh?" He shook his head as he looked at her.

"The line. It's out the door."

"No, uh ..." Unless his father had suddenly developed a lack of pride in appearances, that truck was way too dirty to belong to a Howl. Still, why take chances? "I just remembered my dog." Which wasn't exactly a lie. "My original plan was to grab take-out and then head home to him." But truth be told, Cris had texted him only a half hour ago to say Hercules had gone for an early evening run and been fed. The dog was probably sawing satisfied zzzs right now and could be left for a little bit.

"Okay. Well, then I'll eat at the bar with my friends. Just drop me off at home." She smiled, but he could've sworn he saw disappointment in her eyes.

He did not want to give up the opportunity to spend a little more time with her, especially if she wanted to be with him. "You could always come back to my place, and we could order in."

"Are you propositioning me?" she asked slyly.

"Yes."

"Finally!" Her giant grin kick-started his heart. "I was beginning to think you really might be gay."

The way he felt for her, not a chance in hell.

They ordered pizza delivery from his car. When he said "thin crust" out of habit, she wrinkled her nose and asked, "Do you guys have Sicilian?"

"Yep," the guy on the other end of the call said.

"We'll take that." She nodded at Carter like she'd done him a favor.

"We'll take that," he confirmed.

When he hung up, she stared at him. "Thin crust? That's how you live it up on a Saturday? Next thing you're going to tell me is that you need to stop off for a six-pack of Ultra."

"Nope. It's already in the fridge."

God, he loved her laugh. He'd missed hearing it up close like this. Catching snippets from across the field or from the back of the bus didn't cut it.

"What kind of beer do you drink?" he asked.

"The darker the better. Although, sometimes I'm feeling a real bite-y IPA."

"What are you feeling tonight?" There was a six-pack shop closer to home.

When she didn't answer right away, he looked at her. She was staring at him. "Lucky." Slowly, she slid a hand up his thigh until her fingers grazed the bulge in his pants.

He liked the sound and feel of that.

•••

Jillian followed Carter into a shiny, silver elevator. She felt jittery, like she was either ready to run or make a big mistake. One look at him, and she saw the same uncertainty in his eyes.

"Maybe this was a bad idea," she said.

He simply nodded, maintaining his distance.

"I mean, let's confront the issue head on." She threw his words back at him with a cocky grin. "We aren't really coming here to eat pizza and drink beer."

He considered her, and then he made a fast move, reaching forward and hitting a button that set an alarm blaring. She jumped when the elevator stopped, but she didn't have time to do much more before he pinned her against the wall with nothing but his mouth. Hot and hungry. By the time he dragged his lips away from hers, her head was spinning, her legs were shaking, and she was gripping the brass railing so hard her palms burned.

He punched the same red button, sending the elevator climbing again. "We're going to do whatever the hell we want to do," he said with a smile that trumped any uncertainty. "It's Saturday night."

Her new favorite day of the week.

He grabbed her hand again as they walked the gleaming silver and blue hallway in silence. Her anxiety grew. They couldn't hop in the car and drive away from whatever happened next. They couldn't leave it behind like she'd tried to do with the feelings that had bombarded her in Charity. They were going to have to live with this. She could—she'd lived with much worse. But what about him?

Carter opened the door at the end of the hall and waved her into his condo. It was big, beautiful, and clean. A lot of white. A lot of stone. A lot of steel. A curving staircase that seemed to rise into the clouds ran along floor-to-ceiling windows with a view of the lighted city that made her swoon. She was about to be a smart ass and say she expected something grander when a German shepherd bounded down the stairs, making a beeline straight for her.

"Sit!" Carter commanded, and the dog obeyed.

Jillian jumped, then whistled. "Damn. And I thought your practice voice was bad."

He laughed. "It's just a training technique. My niece doesn't like it either. She calls it my Marine voice." He reached into a silver canister on a nearby counter and then said, "Release!"

The dog walked to him for a treat.

"Hercules, this is Jillian. Jillian, Hercules."

"Hey, baby." She held out a hand. "Aren't you pretty?"

He nudged her hand with his wide head, and she dug her fingers into the thick fur on the sides of his neck.

A buzzer sounded.

"Pizza," Carter said, and he hit a button on the wall panel beside the door. "Be right down." Then he smiled at her. "Make yourself at home."

While he was gone, she explored, opening cupboards out of curiosity. His cans were labels out ... and alphabetized. He didn't have a single junk drawer that she could find. His coat closet had labeled baskets for hats, gloves, and scarves. Man, he was anal. Thinking about living with that much order gave her hives. Which was okay. She wasn't interviewing him for a roommate position. After that kiss in the elevator, she just wanted to see him naked.

Carter walked in on her laughing. He had the pizza in his hand and the most beautiful smile on his face. "I could hear you in the hall. What's so funny?"

"Everything," she said with a shake of her head.

He looked at her, as hot and as hard as he'd kissed her ten minutes ago. "How do you feel about cold pizza?"

"I love it," she said.

Chapter Fourteen

Carter wanted this. He needed this. To hell with the rules he held so damn sacred. He kissed Jillian's knuckles as he stepped into his bedroom and brought her around to face him.

"We play by my rules tonight," she said, as she shoved her hands beneath his shirt and lifted it over his head.

He regarded her with skepticism. "I was just thinking about how I don't want any rules."

"Tough." She brushed her open mouth over the skin at the base of his neck, and his body blissfully hardened. "Consider it payback for the way you treated me at practice." Her soft hands skimmed his sides.

"You know why I had to do that," he said in shallow breaths.

"Uh, uh, uh." She pressed a palm to his mouth. "Rule number one. You talk only when I give you permission to."

He swiped his tongue over her hand and between her fingers until he sucked the tip into his mouth. Her breathing hitched, and her brown eyes melted.

"Rule number two," she whispered. "I'm on the pill, but you will still use protection. If you don't have any, I do." She grinned as she pulled her finger from his mouth and traced it over the bend of his chin and down the length of his neck. "Rule number three. And this is the most important." She pushed onto her toes and pressed her lips to his ear. "What I say goes ... or I go. Nod if we're clear."

He nodded and smoothed his hands down her back to the hem of her shirt, peeling it up and over her head.

She looked at him, eyes sparkling. "Get on the bed." With one arm wrapped behind her back, she dropped her bra to the floor.

His pulse jumped as he took in the sight of her naked from the waist up. What had she just told him to do? Whatever it was, couldn't he touch her first? Couldn't he suck one perfect breast into his mouth until she moaned? That sounded like the best idea to him.

She wiggled out of her pants and underwear.

Couldn't he fall to his knees, open her legs, and …

"Get on the bed, Howl." Her voice was considerably louder now, and the authority was a surprising turn-on.

He obeyed, while she crossed the room and opened doors. If the view wasn't so fine, he might've wondered more about what she was up to.

"Found it," she said as she switched on his closet light and disappeared.

Found what? There was a twinge of worry that came with the question.

She reappeared with two neckties, and he tensed. "No. No way."

"I didn't give you permission to speak," she said. "Besides, you have no idea what I'm going to do with them. Maybe I'm just going to wear them." She dragged one around her neck and let the ends fall between her beautiful breasts. "It looks good, doesn't it?"

His mouth watered. *Very good.* Good enough to make him follow her silly rules.

She crawled onto the bed, her breasts swinging alluringly as she moved.

Mm. He relaxed the slightest bit.

"Don't be scared." She straddled him, settling until his erection fit snuggly between her legs. "I'll be as gentle with you as you were with me at practice this week." She laughed and leaned forward, dangling her breast in front of his mouth.

He opened wide and feasted. Didn't even care when she laced her fingers with his. Couldn't think straight once she started rocking her hips. And when the back of his right hand hit the cold metal bed frame above him, it was too late.

"Relax," she said when he tensed. "You're going to like it."

One more well-placed grind of her hips, and he couldn't argue.

She tied his wrists to the headboard good and tight, and he felt a squeeze in his chest, but it was nothing compared to the squeezing in his groin.

"You're breathing hard," she whispered in his ear.

Ya think? But before he could succumb to the growing lust and panic, she slid down his legs and licked a circle around his naval. He squirmed.

"Aw, you're ticklish. That's cute."

He shook his head back and forth, tugged on the restraints, and tensed against another sweep of her tongue.

He wanted to be in control. He wanted to touch her everywhere. With his hands then his mouth.

She unbuttoned and unzipped his pants, and his thoughts evaporated. The release in pressure felt good, so good his muscles finally softened. Her tongue touched his nipple, then her teeth. Softly, gently.

His heart raced. His blood thickened. He couldn't seem to get enough air to his lungs. But he felt alive, so alive he groaned.

She brushed a chaste kiss across his lips, and ordered him to lift up his hips so she could remove his pants.

He lifted before she finished her sentence.

"Good boy."

That grin. It was half angel, half devil, and he wasn't sure which one was undressing him. He craved them both and tugged on the restraints again.

"Settle down," she said, but then she licked her way up his erection. "Do you have condoms close by?"

"Dresser drawer," he almost begged.

She deep-throated him, gave his balls a little squeeze, and then ran her teeth along his length.

He hissed a breath. *Damn it!* There was so much pressure between his legs. Even more at his wrists. And it extended into his head and chest. "Uncle," he choked out.

"That's not how it works." She laughed, and that sound ... He squeezed his eyes shut. It was not helping.

She stroked him. Everywhere. Coaxing growls from deep inside of him. He was damn near close to begging. But then she was gone, moving across the room in a shadow, and he would've done anything to bring her back, to have her touching him again, wherever, however. Just put him out of his glorious misery. She could call every shot for the rest of his life for all he cared.

That thought startled him more than a little bit.

Then he heard a drawer open, and the telltale sound of a cardboard box rustling in her hands. When her shadow moved closer, he felt damn near euphoric.

"Oh good, you're still here," she said with a soft chuckle.

He pulled against the restraints again, only because he wanted to hold her to his chest and laugh with her. But in an instant, the laughter scattered. She ripped open the packet, and he held his breath.

Her touch was soft and light where he wanted it hard, and she was slow, so painstakingly slow, when he wanted it fast, but every nerve ending stood at attention, ready to drive him over the edge the minute she gave him permission.

With the condom in place and her palms planted on his shoulders, she hovered above him. "I told you it would be fun."

He didn't know what to call it, until she pushed onto him, and he filled her. The sensations ripped a groan from his chest. She lifted slowly at first, up and down, and then her pace quickened. A vicious need overwhelmed him. He wanted her breasts. He wanted her mouth. He wanted all of her. But he was at her mercy entirely.

"Mmm." She leaned in and planted a kiss on his nose, his chin, and then finally his lips.

He took what she gave like he was starving. Their mouths matched the frenetic pace of their bodies grinding together. Amid the heavy breathing, random moaning, and skin slapping, he called her name as he climaxed.

Son of a bitch …

He was spent, destroyed, overruled. And he'd loved every minute of it.

• • •

Jillian reached up and untied him, then she settled onto his chest and listened to his breathing return to a slow, peaceful pace. She ran her fingernails over the curve of his broad shoulder and down his strong left arm, and her own breathing calmed.

He didn't say anything for the longest time, just stroked her lower back and butt with his right hand. So she listened to his heart beating, and figured any minute now, it would start feeling awkward. Being here. Sleeping with him. She didn't even have her car for a clean getaway.

But the awkwardness never came.

They showered and shared cold pizza and beer. Then they curled up on his ginormous white sectional with an exceptionally breathtaking view of the city. Lights twinkled until they were swallowed by the huge black swath of lake in the distance.

"See, this is why I don't do carbs." He was sprawled out across the chaise longue, an arm flung over his eyes. "I crash."

They had the opposite effect on her, but she snuggled in tighter to his warm right side. "That's not the carbs. That's because it's past your bedtime."

"True," he said chuckling.

She traced a figure eight in the light sprinkle of downy hair on his chest. "So now what?"

"We sleep."

"It's 10:30 on a Saturday night. Nobody is sleeping."

"I am."

"Fine. I'll give you fifteen minutes to sleep off the carbs, then I'm waking you up again."

"Deal."

When his breathing deepened, she wiggled out of his arms and off the couch. Hercules was sleeping in a dog bed on the opposite side of the room, and she smiled at him. "Just like your daddy. Aren't you?"

But unlike Carter, the dog got up and followed her to the kitchen, where she grabbed another piece of pizza and considered messing up the cupboards just for fun. Instead, she tore off tiny pieces of pizza crust and fed them to Hercules. "Bet you don't get that often, do you?"

From her perch on a stool at the kitchen island, she could still see Carter asleep in the living room. Washed in a ribbon of moonlight and cradled by the snow white couch, he looked like a gender-role-reversed Sleeping Beauty. She guessed that made her the prince, because in—she glanced at the clock on the shiny, metal microwave—ten minutes, she was going to wake him with a kiss.

The prince. She dropped her gaze to her Cinderella tattoo. Fairy tales weren't normally her thing. Happily ever after sounded great, but when she ran into it in real life, it always looked boring as hell. She glanced at Carter again. He was nothing like Keller. But as hot as he was, as rich as he was, as kind as he was, she doubted there was a fairy-tale ending here. They were too damn different, and he was too hung up on his dad's approval.

Jillian hopped off the stool and made her way back into the living room. She was bored, and when she was bored, she thought too much. That's when she got into the most trouble. She needed to find something to do.

Lights from the skyline reflected off a huge black curving rectangle that anchored Carter's media center. She moved closer and estimated the television to be at least 75 inches. Was there a remote? She found three. The first one was too small and light to be the main remote. She put it down and picked up another, squinting in the dim light to read the small print on the buttons.

"Use this."

She smiled at the sleepy voice and then turned to see him sitting up, holding a tablet computer.

"I only use the remotes when I forget to charge this. There's an app to control the lights in the room, too." He tapped the screen, and a soft glow illuminated the crown molding all around them. "See? Mood lighting." His brows bobbed. "Here. Watch what you want."

How 'bout she just watch him sitting there shirtless on the big white couch? That was damn near pornography, but she glanced back at the TV. A gaming system on the lowest shelf caught her eye. She crouched for a better look. "Xbox?"

"PlayStation. Well, PlayStation on steroids. We have these in the restaurants. The memories are so huge, no hard copy game is required. Everything is stored on a server. Do you play?"

"I used to play Xbox a lot." Her old console had gone the way of the red ring of death, and she didn't have the money to replace it. "So much I overheated the thing."

"I can relate." He grinned, and then he leaned forward, opened a hidden drawer in the coffee table, and offered her a black controller. "Want to take it for a spin?"

She leapt to him. "Uh, yeah!"

With a touch of another button on his tablet, the television lit up and the console fan buzzed.

She curled a leg beneath her and sat beside him, remote in hand. "Do you have *Madden*?"

"Honey, I have *everything*."

She whooped. "I've officially died and gone to heaven."

He gave her a slow, sultry look. "The heaven part can be arranged."

"Oh yeah?"

"Oh yeah." He leaned into her until their mouths met and she was lying beneath him.

She dropped the controller to the floor. "I'm going back to that later."

"Much later," he whispered against her neck.

A happy sigh left her lips. She'd take an evening like this over the fairy tale any day.

Chapter Fifteen

The next morning, Jillian didn't know what hit her. She woke up in Carter's bed, in Carter's arms, after a night that on the surface, had been literally fun and games. But it shook her to the core. Made her feel ... edgy. In the light of day, he looked edgy, too. Unshaven. Underdressed. Sexy as sin, but the uncertainty had returned in his eyes.

"Let's get you back to your car," he said.

But first, she needed to get her keys. Jade always went to 11:30 Sunday services with her family, so now was as good a time as any.

The ride was quiet, calm, and she fidgeted most of the way. "So is this like the drive of shame?"

He glanced at her. "I don't know. You tell me. Are you embarrassed by what happened last night?"

"No." She rolled her eyes. "I don't embarrass easily."

He smiled—finally—and she settled a bit. "I know."

"We had fun. Fun is good."

"Yep ..."

She could sense the "but" before he even said it. "But?"

He glanced at her. "We need to keep it quiet."

Back to his dad again. But she'd known all about that last night when she'd agreed to get into this car. "Then I will make you pay for my silence in orgasms."

He laughed and grabbed her hand to kiss her knuckles. Her eyelids fluttered a tiny bit. In some ways, that felt even more intimate than sex. The thought rattled her. Was she getting in too deep? She faced her window and rolled her eyes. Never.

The closer they got to her apartment, the more unsettled she became. "Drop me off here," she said.

He looked at her like she was crazy. "We're a good three blocks away."

"I'll walk, and then I'll have someone else drive me out to get my car. We need to keep it quiet, right?"

His face wrinkled. "Yeah, but I don't like dropping you off and not knowing if you got home okay."

"Oh my God. You sound like Jade. I'll be fine. I'll even text when I get home as a onetime courtesy."

He pulled into the drugstore parking lot then hit a button on his steering wheel. "Call Jillian," he said.

Her phone buzzed in her hand.

"Answer it," he said. "And talk to me until you get home."

She accepted the call and raised the phone to her ear. "You're bossy," she said.

"Says the woman who tied me to the headboard."

Oh, that made her laugh. She was still laughing off and on as she turned the corner and headed in the direction of her place.

"Where are you now?" he asked.

"Same place. I'm walking, not running."

"Walk faster," he said. Then he chuckled and asked, "You're walking slower now, aren't you?"

"Yep. Next time maybe you should try reverse psychology."

"What the hell are you doing?" asked another voice.

She'd been so distracted by Carter she didn't hear a car pull up beside her. Tanya and MJ.

Shit. "Why aren't you in Detroit?"

"Early flight," Tanya said.

"Go," Carter said in her ear.

She ended the call as nonchalantly as possible.

"Everything okay?" MJ asked.

"Yep. Wanna give me a ride?" Jillian was already opening the backdoor of MJ's SUV.

The car started moving, and Tanya started interrogating. "So, where ya headed back from?"

"The pharmacy." Which was not a lie, not technically. They'd been in the pharmacy lot when she got out of Carter's car.

"Condoms, tampons, or chocolate?" MJ asked.

She looked out the window and squeezed her eyes shut. She did not like to lie to them. "I didn't buy anything."

"Were you by chance looking for these?" Tanya was dangling Jillian's keys over the front seat.

"Why would my keys be at the pharmacy?" She took them from Tanya's hand. "Thank you. I forgot I put them in your bag. Good thing I have another set, huh?"

MJ pulled into Mama Mary's lot.

"You do have another set," Tanya said. "And yet, where's your car?" The spot where Jillian usually parked was woefully empty.

"At the stadium." She opened the car door. "Thanks for the ride, MJ."

"Jill, not so fast." MJ put the vehicle in park but didn't unlock the doors before turning to face her. "Gloria Eberly saw you leave the stadium with Carter Howl."

Big deal. At least Gloria wasn't Coach Howl.

Tanya turned all the way around in her seat. "When MJ picked me up at the airport and told me that, I already knew I had your keys, so I figured he just gave you a ride home to get your other keys. But now, here you are in the same clothes I saw you in after the game, and here your car isn't. Which makes me think ... things. I thought you said you were going out with the band last night."

MJ nodded. "That's what you said."

Jillian huffed an exhale. "You guys. That was the plan, but then I asked Carter for a ride, and plans changed."

"What kind of ride are we talking here?" Tanya asked.

Jillian laughed. She had to. She always did when Tanya's voice went all low and full of attitude.

"Did you do more than kissing last night?" MJ asked point blank. There wasn't a hint of amusement on her face.

Jillian looked away. "It's no big deal." God, she was saying it so much it was starting to lose its punch.

MJ faced the steering wheel and dropped her head to the headrest. "Do you not see what's going on with this team? You and Carter are manic. One day, you're yelling at each other. The next day, you're ignoring each other. And somehow, the rest of us are supposed to just deal with it."

Jillian pressed her fingers to her temples. "It's not *that* bad." Was it?

But Tanya seemed to be confirming it with a nod.

"Whatever." Jillian hopped out of the car with a force that jostled her. "Thanks for the ride."

"Wait." Tanya was out of the car, too. "We're just worried one or both of you will end up kicked off the team. Coach Howl doesn't look happy, you know?"

Oh, she knew. "That won't happen as long as we stay quiet. We just have to keep it from his father, and everything will be alright. As far as Gloria is concerned, Carter took me home to get my keys. Okay? And I promise ..." she reached into the car through Tanya's open door and grabbed onto MJ's arm, "I promise it won't affect the team." She slid her hand down until she hand MJ's pinky linked with hers.

"Already has," MJ said stonily.

"Girl, you worry me," Tanya said. "This time you're playing with serious fire, and you don't even realize it. Since when do you sneak around? The Jillian I know would've marched right up to Coach Howl a long time ago and told him he couldn't control what she did off the field, as long as she produced on Game Day."

True. She'd done it many times when it came to partying. But ... "This is different."

"You need to take a good, hard look in the mirror and ask yourself why it's different. Because girl, if you expect Thor to choose you over his daddy, you're going to get burned. And burns like that don't heal."

Jillian glanced at her tattoo. Everything healed. She was living proof.

...

Standing outside Amanda's house less than two hours after he'd dropped Jillian off felt surreal and incredibly deceitful knowing his father was here. The front door opened. "Uncle Carter!" Sophia threw her arms around his waist. "You came."

"What do you mean I came? Of course I came. I'm always here on Sunday."

"Not last Sunday." She pulled back and studied him. "Where were you?"

"With a friend." He shoved the uncomfortable topic aside and stepped into the house. "Where is everyone? Kitchen?"

She nodded. "And Pop Pop's in the den. Were you with Cris?"

He shook his head. She knew Cris mostly because of the rare occasions when Carter traveled for work and Cris kept up with taking pictures of Hercules. "Nope. Not Cris. Someone else. Now, let's talk about something different. You played sharp this week. Nice jump shot."

"I don't have a jump shot yet," she said. "Were you with a girl someone else?"

He sighed. "Kiddo, you ask too many questions."

"Bro!" Russ appeared at the end of the hallway with the baby on his hip. "Glad to see you made it."

Carter threw up his hands. "What is with you guys? It was one Sunday. Cripes." He shook his head as he tweaked his nephew's nose and walked past Russ into the kitchen.

"Aha!" Amanda said. "The prodigal son returns."

He snatched a carrot stick off the island. "You, too?"

"Nah." She took a bowl from Ruthie, who was tending to a wiggly Katherine. "We heard Russ ragging you, so we thought we'd join in. It's fun to get you all riled up."

"Where'd you go?" Ruthie asked. She'd been out the night he'd helped Russ move furniture, which had seemed like a blessing at the time. He should've anticipated a later round of questioning.

"Pennsylvania."

"Was it for work?" Amanda said.

He scrolled through his memory, trying to remember if he'd gotten specific with his brother. If Carter had, Russ may have told his wife and sister.

"He was with a girl someone," Sophia said.

Amanda and Ruthie suddenly had matching wide eyes and open mouths.

Carter backed toward the den. "She's speculating. She didn't get that from me." He shot his niece a loving but firm "keep your lips zipped" look.

She stuck out her tongue.

Carter joined his father and Nick in the den, where they were watching NASCAR. Racing wasn't his thing, but it was better than taking the heat in the kitchen. Besides, he needed some quiet to come up with a plan. He had a feeling the ladies weren't going to let this die. Maybe he could pull Amanda aside, be honest with her, and ask her to run interference for him.

"Did you go to Pennsylvania with a girl?" Russ stood in the doorway to the dining room, looking incredulous.

Nick looked at Carter. Dad, too, and the look on Dad's face was murderous.

Fuck. "None of your business."

"Ooh. Why so salty?" Russ asked. "I'm just curious. Some of us may or may not have money riding on when and if you settle down."

Ass.

"He said it's none of your goddamn business." Dad's brisk tone startled everyone.

"Okay. Sorry. Geez," Russ said. "I'll back off, man."

Carter didn't want this tension. "I was helping a friend," he said. "She needed an escort to a family thing. That's it."

Russ nodded.

"Always so chivalrous," Nick said. "Those Marine commercials with the swords have a knight in shining armor feel for a reason, don't they?"

Everybody but Carter and his father were laughing.

"Are you done?" his father snapped. "I'd like to watch the race."

Russ shot a disgusted look at their father. "Hey, Nick, how 'bout helping me put leaves into the table."

When the other guys left the room, the air crackled with an uncomfortable silence, and Carter stood to leave, too.

"Happy now?" his father asked. "You got the whole damn family worked up over this, just like the team."

What a gross exaggeration. He wasn't going to acknowledge it with an answer.

But then his father looked at him. "You're probably thinking, 'Who the hell cares? I'm a man. I can do what I want to do. If things don't work out with the team, I can walk away. I still have my business.' None of it's a big deal to you, right? Just like running off to join the Marines was no big deal to you. You seem to forget you leave people behind who have to live with your decisions." He shook his head.

"You think I wanted to leave you and the family? I joined the Marines *because* of my family. Because when Sophia was born, I wanted this world to be a safer place. I wanted her to be able to grow up with the same piece of mind I'd had, until, well ... until Mom died." His father's hardened expression wavered the slightest bit, but he didn't say anything to soften the moment. Carter shook his head. "Dad, I know you were disappointed I didn't go into the NFL, but I thought I was doing the right thing. I still do."

"Disappointed? It wasn't disappointment over you walking away from a professional career, boy! It was worry for your life so damn thick I couldn't sleep." His father's thunderous voice broke painfully. "And just a couple years after losing your mother? How did you expect me to react?"

Just like that, Carter thought. He hadn't wanted to believe that his decision to enlist had been anything but courageous and inspired, but now he knew it really had been selfish, too.

After a lengthy exhale, Carter nodded. "I'm very sorry I ever caused you to worry, but I'm here now. I came back. So why is there still this overriding feeling that I'm disappointing you at every turn? With my personal life. With the team."

"The team is all I have," his father blurted. "Coaching is the only dream I ever had—for myself," he added bitterly. "One e-mail about coach and player impropriety could bring the league down on me, and just like that ..." he snapped his fingers, "I could lose it all. Would you think about what your actions were doing to me then?"

Race sounds filled the room on the heels of his father's heavy silence. Carter stood there, reeling. He did not want his father to lose that team. He did not want to hurt the man with any more of his actions. He didn't want to hurt Jillian, either. But after everything his father just said, Carter didn't have a choice.

Chapter Sixteen

By lunch on Monday, Carter had composed two dozen different texts he never sent to Jillian, and his thumb was cramped from hovering over the call button. He needed to tell her they were finished, this thing between them had run its course. But every time he thought of the words, his mind and body revolted. He worried it might never be over as long as they were in contact. So he set his phone aside yet again, and focused on his grilled chicken salad.

A half-hour later with his salad still untouched, he decided he needed to get out of there. He wanted a juicy burger on a big, fat brioche bun and a craft beer. Maybe the carb load would help dull the pain of cutting Jillian loose.

Once he was out on the street in the afternoon sun, he finally texted her, intending to invite her along so they could talk, and he could end this game. She invited him to her place instead, saying Jade was at work and she had Double Stuf Oreos. He told himself the private location was better in case she got upset.

It took all of ten minutes for them to end up in bed.

"This was not what I came for," he said in a husky voice while he planted kisses on her neck.

"I know," she whispered, her hands making short work of his dress pants. "You came for the junk food. It's okay. Admit it."

He didn't need any more junk food. He needed her. But it was no longer okay to admit that.

•••

Jillian didn't press him for information about why he'd really come. *This* was better than any other reason that could've brought him here.

She kept her mouth shut and her hands above his waist, wanting to prolong everything. Every brush of his lips. Every slide of his hands. Every shared breath. He was glorious. She adored the way his back muscles flexed while he was undressing her and the way his soft head of hair tickled her palms. With her eyes closed, she memorized every detail amid an unexplainable fear that had grown too big to ignore. He'd come to end it.

But first, this. Carter dragged his lips lower, over her stomach, her hip bone, her thigh, and then he took her with his mouth, banishing her thoughts. He flicked his tongue back and forth, up and down. She lifted her hips, and called his name. Closer and closer he pushed her until she was tumbling over the edge. Delicious.

He stayed there, loving her, until the tremors subsided. "Yum," she said. The mattress shifted as he moved back up her body, and his breath tickled her face. She opened her eyes and smiled. "You're very good at that."

His laugh was low and mostly air. "You inspire me."

He looked so happy. Maybe she'd been wrong. Maybe nothing was going to change between them. But the longer he looked at her, the more serious his expression became, and then he kissed her—like only he could. Soul deep. And her heart cramped.

She reached between his legs and played until he broke off the kiss with a glorious guttural sound.

"Condom." She pulled out the packet she'd stashed beneath her pillow.

It was on in a flash, and he was inside of her just as quickly. Thrust after thrust rattled her senses. She wrapped her legs around him, pulling him closer, taking him deeper. He groaned, his lips against her temple and then they were on her lips. Hot and fierce. She swallowed every exhale, cushioned every blow, and when he collapsed on top of her—completely spent—she held him there, closed her eyes, and heard three little words roar through her brain. *I love you.*

It was true. No wonder she'd been scared.

He rolled off of her, planted a kiss between her breasts, and disappeared into the bathroom across the hall. She loved him even though he wanted rules and order, while she wanted fun and freedom. Because when they were together, it felt like she had everything. Fun and stability. A friend and a lover. *Mm.* That last one. She curled up beneath the covers, and mentally replayed the last twenty minutes of bliss.

Then the bathroom door opened, and Carter came out and simply said, "We have to stop."

"What?" She sat up, tugging the blanket over her chest. "What are you talking about?"

"My father says it's affecting the team and my family." He slipped into his boxers, then his dress pants. "I don't know. Maybe it is."

That's what Tanya had said. But Jillian didn't want to believe it. Odds were, he was just caving to his dad. Again. She made a face.

"My dad said the league comes down hard on sexual harassment claims. He says one e-mail about coach and player impropriety could cause him to lose the franchise. This team is his dream." Carter sat on the edge of the bed and smoothed a hand up the outline of her leg. "I can't be the reason he loses another dream. Do you understand?"

Ooh. She was going to be sick, physically sick. Of course, she understood! Tanya had been right again. He was picking his father over her. Like it should be, she told herself, but she still felt hollow inside—and defensive. "I would never cry sexual harassment or send an e-mail to the league. That's crazy. I've been an active participant in this!"

He roughed his other hand over his mouth. "I know, but someone else could."

"Carter, that doesn't make any sense. If someone else complains about being sexually harassed by you, then they're lying. An investigation would prove that."

He nodded. "Maybe. Maybe not. But it doesn't matter. I can't take that risk."

Because he didn't feel like she did. He didn't love her. She looked away, and her disgust turned to white hot anger. "Get out!"

He looked at her. The hurt in his eyes was almost enough to make her believe he felt something pretty damn close. "We should talk about this. I don't want it to affect the team."

Of course he didn't. Forget about how it affected her. She narrowed her eyes at him. "I thought you said you wouldn't run away."

He broke eye contact. "That was ... This is ... different." But he didn't bother explaining how.

"Get out," she said again, giving him a shove off the bed this time.

He picked up the rest of his clothes and managed an "I'm sorry" before he left her room.

"Fucking coward!" she yelled after him.

She would've been willing to fight her family for him.

• • •

Ending things with Jillian was the right thing, but it felt all wrong. The sting from the words she'd hurled at him while he was walking down her hall never dulled. He wasn't a coward, and he resented being called that.

He spent the rest of the week submerged in things that were supposed to take his mind off Jillian. He worked. He ran the dog. He cleaned the kitchen. He reorganized his closets. And when football practices rolled around, he kept his distance, which ended up being surprisingly easy now that Rooney was having pain in her arm and he was tapped to spend practice working with her. However, easy was not the word he would use to describe Rooney's demeanor toward him. It seemed Jillian's hostility was contagious.

Before Carter knew it, the weekend arrived, and he boarded the bus for the trip to Cincinnati. Even with all the chatter, he could zero in on her laughter without ever turning his head. Four hours of that beautiful sound would be the end of him. Fortunately, he came prepared. He slid a pair of studio quality headphones on and cranked up the tunes, skipping every Harvey Danger song that came through the rotation.

A few hours into the trip, Carter's father yanked on his sleeve. "How's Rooney's arm?" The question was rude and demanding, just like every word his father had said to him this week.

No idea. Rooney—and Martin and Wren—had been glued to Jillian's side, so he'd been avoiding them. "I'll talk to her once we get there."

When Carter stepped off the bus in Cincinnati, he saw an opportunity to corner Rooney while she was alone. As usual, she looked less than thrilled.

"How's the arm?" he asked.

"Fine." She couldn't make eye contact with him. Either she was lying about the arm, or it was her newfound hate for him.

"Pain or no pain."

"No pain."

"Good. Maybe the drills are working."

She made a face. "Or maybe it's because I took Advil."

"Sure. That helps." Clearing the air between them might help, too. What did he have to lose? He took a big breath. "Rooney, I know you know."

Her eyes widened for a split second.

"You have every right to be pissed," he continued. "I made some dick moves. They were unintentional and totally out of character, but that's beside the point. My actions put the team at risk, and I'm truly sorry for that. I'm trying to fix it. I swear. I want to do right by all of you. My father, too."

Rooney glared at him. "But not Jillian."

"No! That's not what I meant." He wanted to do right by Jillian, too. He just didn't know how to make everyone happy. "I want her to be okay most of all."

Rooney looked downright incredulous. "So you hurt her."

"I didn't mean to. I was backed into a corner. Believe me ..." The words caught in his throat. "I wish there'd been another way." He raised a hand to God.

Rooney seemed to study him with a smidge less hostility now, but when she opened her mouth, it was back. "Are we done yet?"

He supposed. There wasn't much more he could say. He'd done the right thing as far as his father and the team were concerned. But his Dad was still mad. MJ was still mad. God knew Jillian probably wanted his head—both heads—on a spike.

What the hell was the incentive for playing by the rules if it made everyone miserable?

•••

Saturday's win against Cincinnati had been the highlight of what Jillian had dubbed the F.A.W.—"fucking awful week." While it was nice to know harmony could still exist on the football field, off the field, everything was a mess. Her friends vacillated between coddling her like she was a psych case and pulling out the tough-love "I told you sos." Her bands kept saying she'd changed, that she wasn't as much fun anymore. Her head coach looked at her like she wore a freaking scarlet letter. And Carter ... fucking Carter. She missed him. Desperately. That sort of weakness would not—could not—be tolerated, so she pretended like she didn't care.

On Monday, Jillian walked from the parking lot to the locker room with Jade by her side. She caught a glimpse of Carter talking to Coach Riggles by the soda machines, and that stupid flutter in her chest stole her breath.

Don't care. Don't care. But seeing him wasn't getting any easier.

Jade hooked an arm through Jillian's and quickened the pace.

"My mother says men are like a box of chocolate; you're not always going to like what you find inside, and nobody wants them after they've been tasted."

Jillian laughed. "What the hell does that even mean?"

"No idea. But it made you laugh."

Jillian was just about to laugh again when her phone buzzed. Seeing Wendy's name wiped the smile from her face. An ominous feeling replaced everything else. "You go in. I have to take this."

She took a breath before she answered. "Hello?"

"Jillie, I'm scared. The doctors want Caleb to go to Cleveland Clinic to be assessed for the surgery. That's not far from you, is it?"

"No, it's close, and it's good. The best."

Wendy's exhale echoed. "That's what Bob said. He checked it out online, but I wanted to hear it from you. Remember all those times when you told me Dad was going to kick the bad guy in the …" she lowered her voice, "ass, and come home okay. Well, you were right. You were always right."

Jillian smiled and battled a surge of emotion. "It's going to be okay, Wendy. It's going to be just like that this time, too. This is good for Caleb. It's one step closer to getting him better."

"Thank you. That really does make me feel better. We'll be there this weekend. Friday through Monday. That way, they can see him twice before they send us home. It helps that I get to see you, too. Did you get a ring?"

Oh, sweet Jesus. The stupid fake engagement. "No. Wendy …"

"Maybe we could go looking while I'm there. That would be an awesome way to take my mind off all the worry! Don't you think?"

Jillian banged her forehead gently off the brick building. "I suppose. But I'm not sure I'll have time. Friday, I have practice and then a band I have to see. Saturday I have a game."

"I want to come to your game!"

"Bob will never come to my game."

"I can convince him. He's been a lot more attentive since you and Carter were here."

Well, at least everything hadn't been a bust.

"We'll spend Sunday afternoon together at least," Wendy said. "And then dinner! Bob, me, and Caleb with you and Carter."

Shit. "Wendy." But again, Jillian hesitated. Her sister had sounded miserable when the conversation began. Now, she sounded hopeful. Jillian didn't want to rob her of that just to sweep her conscience clean. "I don't think he'll be able to make it Sunday."

"Oh, no. Why?"

"He has other plans."

"I bet you have ways to get him to cancel." She giggled.

Not anymore, Jillian thought.

"Listen, I'll talk to him," she said. At this point, she was desperate to end the call.

There was no way Carter would agree to play the part of a happy couple again. No way.

So why did she keep trying to think up ways to ask him?

• • •

Carter left the stadium a little later than usual. MJ had asked him to take a closer look at some footwork and timing issues she'd been struggling with. He'd been happy to impart every ounce of wisdom he'd gained as a D-1 QB. He'd been even happier she'd come to him, willingly. That conversation in Cincinnati must've helped.

His phone vibrated in his hand with a text from Cris: *Yoga instructor brought a friend. Interested?*

No thanks, he texted back. Tonight he was going home to Hercules and a half-eaten package of Oreos. He would be drooling on his pillow by ten, probably with the dog sleeping beside him.

You're missing out, buddy.

Carter didn't exactly doubt that. But no matter how he looked at it, he just wasn't interested. Maybe next week.

A few feet from his car, he heard running behind him, and then a breathy, "Carter."

He turned to see Jillian striding toward him and had the most ridiculous impulse to open his arms and give her a soft place to land. He shoved his hands in his pockets instead.

She briefly made eye contact with him. "Wendy and Bob are bringing Caleb to Cleveland Clinic on Friday. They're staying the weekend."

The collection of words was the largest she'd spoken to him since the day she'd called him a coward. That still hurt. And as much as he wanted to defend himself and his decision now, he refrained. "Is everything okay with the baby?" he asked.

She nodded. "Wendy wants me and you to go to dinner with them on Sunday. I know it's crazy, but ..."

So she was still hanging on to the charade? A brief second of ridiculous relief that at least they were still together in some alternate universe gave way to disappointment as reality came crashing in.

"I haven't had a chance to tell them ..." she looked away again, "about us yet. I don't want to do it now while she's worried about Caleb, so this is just a heads up, because they might be at the game Saturday. I'm thinking over Bob's dead body, but ... anyway." She swiped a hand through the air between them, and disgust registered on her face. "Never mind. This was a bad idea." She started to back away.

"Jillian ..." When he said her name, she looked at him—really looked at him—and he could've sworn he saw something other than loathing in her eyes.

He pulled a hand from his pocket and reached for her, but at that same moment, he caught sight of his father leaving the stadium a few yards away.

Carter dropped his hand and put more space between them. "Tell them I have an important dinner with out-of-town clients. That way Bob won't feel too smug." He couldn't live with himself if he allowed that. "In fact, feel free to text me when you get to dinner, and I'll play along."

"For legitimacy's sake," she said, her mouth twisted.

His father was coming toward them, probably thinking the worst. Or maybe that was Carter's paranoia talking. After all, his father's car was parked three spaces away. The man had to come toward them if he wanted to go home.

"I have to go," Carter whispered.

He opened his door, sat inside his car, and watched her head back toward the field. At one point, she crossed paths with his father. She actually stopped, and the pair exchanged words. The interaction didn't seem to last long enough for it to be much more than "good night" and "see you tomorrow." But it had a profound impact on him, the man who sought refuge in his car.

He really was acting like a coward, wasn't he?

Chapter Seventeen

It was always a battle when New York came to town. They were big and fast, two things that didn't always go together, two things that made a wide receiver's job that much harder. But Jillian had reason to play harder than she ever had before—Wendy and Bob were actually here. She looked up into the stands and smiled at her sister, who was wearing Caleb in a quilted sling, then she glanced at Bob. *Ready for a show, dickwad?*

MJ clapped to break the huddle, and the game was underway. Three running plays, three consecutive first downs. New York might be big and fast, but they were holey. And when MJ hit her in the back of the end zone on only the fourth play of the game, Jillian knew it was going to be a great game.

From then on, the ball came to her deftly and often. Her feet felt like they barely touched the ground, and by halftime, Jillian had 70 receiving yards under her belt. She'd said it was going to be great, but she'd been wrong. It was going to be epic. Maybe Wendy was her good luck charm.

Running into the locker room at the half, she had her heart set on a record-breaking game. Nothing she heard from Coach made her think anything would change, but New York made adjustments in the third. Their refocused speed and coverage shut down Jillian, frustrating her play after play and nearly causing an interception. The writing was on the wall even before Carter started pulling pass plays: The Clash would be running the ball until further notice. So much for her record-breaking game. It festered at first, making her miserable in the huddle, but when she looked at her teammates, she remembered why she was here. To have fun. With them. And to win football games. She was going to take her fun where she could find it, and that meant blocking like a beast.

After throwing a flawless and legal crackback block, which yielded them impressive rushing yards, Jillian forgot all about the throwing and catching part. And when MJ scrambled into the end zone for a touchdown, Jillian felt the joy as if she'd crossed the plain herself.

"Textbook block," Carter said with a smile when she reached the sideline.

"Thanks." The fact that he was the kind of guy who could recognize that made him even more attractive, but she immediately killed the thought and jogged away.

The clock continued to run down, until they were facing the two-minute warning. The ball hadn't come her way once in the fourth quarter. And when MJ took a knee to claim another Clash win, Jillian was thrilled to be a part of it. She whooped her way to the sidelines, smacking her teammates on the ass, looking for everyone and anyone to share the joy with. And there was Carter, watching her, wearing the biggest smile on his face. He was the one she wanted to run to, to share her joy with, but she tempered her enthusiasm.

"Jillie!"

Wendy's voice came from somewhere over by the fence.

Jillian ran to her. "What did you think of that?" She wrapped her hands around the chainlink and leaned over for a peek at the baby. Somehow he was sleeping through all the chaos.

"It was amazing!" Wendy said. "I can't believe you run that fast."

Jillian laughed. "Did you see the size of some of those linebackers? You would run fast, too."

Bob lurked in the background. He didn't look nearly as impressed as her sister was, but at least he'd brought Wendy here.

Maybe that was progress. Maybe things could be reasonable between them.

"So what did you think, Bob?" Jillian asked.

"I think that's your fiancé over there," he said. And to Jillian's horror, he headed down the chainlink fence toward Carter, Coach Howl, and a smiling little girl.

•••

Carter smiled at Sophia, who was rattling on about girl power and how she liked football now and wanted Carter to teach her to play. Man, his father had never looked prouder.

"Your Uncle Carter can teach you how to throw the ball so good you'll be the greatest female quarterback ever to play the game," the beaming man said.

Apparently, Carter's dad had a new project, and somehow that lifted a great big weight from Carter's shoulders.

"I want a picture of all three of us," Sophia said. "And then I want to get autographs."

Maybe he could grab Jillian. What a kick he'd get out of seeing them together.

"Carter!" A deep and unfamiliar voice drew his attention down the line of fence.

Bob was striding toward him with a goofy smile on his face.

"Who's that?" Sophia asked.

Well now, wasn't this inconvenient?

But as Carter glanced at his niece and then his dad underneath the blazing sun and the aura of a killer win, he realized there wasn't anything Bob could say that would make things any worse than they'd already been. If he couldn't have it all, then the only thing he wanted was Jillian.

Carter met him halfway, still hoping to keep things short and sweet. "Bob ..." he extended a hand, "nice to see you again."

Behind Bob, came Jillian, a mix of fear and fury on her face. "Hey!" she yelled. "Bob, you have to see this." She was in total rescue mode.

All Carter could do was smile. She was so fucking fierce.

"Can I get your autograph?" Sophia's excited voice sounded at Carter's side, and then she held out a notebook and a Sharpie to Jillian.

Jillian looked startled for a minute, and then she smiled. "Of course! What's your name?"

"Sophia. Hey, did that hurt?"

Carter watched in silent awe as Sophia pointed to Jillian's tattoos.

Bob snorted.

Everyone else ignored him.

"It did," Jillian said as she scribbled something in Sophia's book. "A lot. I had to go back over and over again with months in between so it could heal. But I think it was worth it."

Bob snorted again.

"Me, too," Sophia said. "It's really cool. Do you think maybe I could take a picture of it for my Instagram?"

"We can do better than that," Jillian said. She stood behind Sophia and wrapped the tattooed arm across the child's chest. Then she hunched down so their faces were aligned, and with her free arm extended, snapped a picture of them with Sophia's phone.

Sophia beamed as she looked back and forth between the picture and Jillian. "Oh that is so cool. So cool! It doesn't even need a filter. Uncle Carter! Look at this."

Both Jillian and Bob gaped. Wendy, who had just walked up, looked confused.

Carter smiled at his niece. "It's great, Soph. Best picture I've ever seen. In fact, send that to me so I can make it my background." He looked at Jillian and tried to smile away her shock.

"There's no way you're engaged!" Bob said. "She doesn't even know his niece." He directed that jab at Wendy.

Jillian reached for her sister, who seemed to understand now. Carter reached for Jillian.

"You're engaged?" Sophia asked. A flash of confusion turned to excitement.

Carter's father picked that moment to finish the walk over to them. "Who's engaged?" he asked.

Over top Jillian's attempt to explain things to Wendy, Carter yelled, "I am."

He finally caught hold of Jillian's flailing hand and yanked her to him. "I asked her to marry me in her parent's kitchen, and she said yes. Didn't you?"

For once, she was speechless, staring at him like he was certifiably crazy, a little like she had when he'd dropped to one knee in Charity.

But she quickly found her voice. "That wasn't for real."

"Carter, what the hell is going on?" his father asked.

"Language, Pop Pop," Sophia said, and then she laughed. "Oh my God! The tattoo picture already has sixty-five likes!"

Carter didn't care about any of it, but the beautiful, courageous, outrageous woman by his side, and he suddenly, deeply wanted to be worthy of her until the day he died. "I love you," he said.

He watched her jaw drop and felt her body sway.

"I love you," he said again, nodding this time, hoping she would understand that this wasn't just some ruse for appearances' sake. "I refuse to believe love isn't enough to keep us together. To keep us all together," he said to the shocked and confused family members around them. All except Sophia, who ... He glanced at her raised phone, and the smile on her face. Yep, she was totally recording this.

"Is this for real-real?" Jillian asked skeptically.

"Absolutely."

Her hand smoothed its way up his belly to his chest, and her eyes never left his face. "Then in that case ... I love you, too. I'm sorry I ever called you a coward. This took guts."

"Kiss her," Sophia giggled.

"Yes, please!" Wendy echoed.

"Oh, for the love of God," Bob said.

Carter looked at his father, who was surprisingly calm taking things in. "If I need to resign before I do this, I will."

"No!" Jillian said, her hand landing over his heart. "I'll resign before you do."

His father shook his head. "Oh, hell. Kiss the woman, Carter. We'll work out the details later."

"My pleasure," Carter said. He slid a hand to the back of her neck and pulled her into his kiss.

Somewhere behind all the fireworks his body blasted off, he heard Sophia and Wendy laughing.

And then he heard Bob's gruff word, "Unbelievable."

For once, Carter agreed with him.

Epilogue

Carter officially asked Jillian to marry him one week later. After his father had done some research and agreed that an engaged couple wouldn't raise the ire of the league. Apparently Baltimore's owner-coach was married to the starting quarterback. Jillian pointed out that had the Howl men done their research in the first place, they could've saved everyone a lot of trouble. Then she promised to save them from themselves for as long as she lived. That earned her a genuine smile from her future father-in-law and a wild night in bed with her future husband, which may or may not have involved a dog collar and chain.

And now, here they were on the weekend off before playoffs, the same weekend Caleb's surgery had been deemed a success, sitting side by side in tattoo parlor chairs.

Jillian smiled at Carter, who was looking a little pale. "I don't understand what the big deal is. You've done this before."

He shook his head and glanced at the side table where the tattoo artist, Mick, was lining up his equipment. "That doesn't mean I wasn't nervous then. I hate needles."

She laughed. "I'll kiss it and make it better when we get home." The sparkle in his deep blue eyes made her want to crawl onto his chair and kiss him right then and there.

"What'd you finally decide on?" he asked.

Her tattoo artist, Leah, had left the room with the winning sketch a few minutes ago.

"You'll see," she said slyly.

"I don't understand why it's such a big secret. We've been talking about getting tattoos to celebrate the engagement for weeks. I've heard all your ideas."

Except one. This one had come to her the other night as she snuggled next to him in bed, listening to him complain about how the dog never slept with him until she walked into his life and destroyed the order of things with "two measly neckties." She rested her head against the chair and laughed. *Neckties for the win.* There would be two, one striped and one floral, intertwined and wrapping around her left wrist, so as not to compete with her existing tattoos.

"Ready?" Mick asked Carter.

"Sure. What the hell. Let's do this," he said.

Jillian grinned as Mick laid out the template she'd helped him create. She liked the way Cinderella's dress had been shortened to just above her knees. She liked the way Thor held her passionately against his chest. But what she absolutely adored was the way Cinderella held Thor's hammer loosely by her side.

"Left arm, correct?" Mick asked.

Carter nodded and reached out with his right to grab Jillian's hand. "You are the only woman in the world who could ever get me to cross a line like this."

God, that was sweet. And the fact that he had the guts to go through with it made her love him even more.

"You know? We've both crossed a lot of lines in the last few months," she said. "Every one of them was worth it as far as I'm concerned."

He seemed to consider that, and then he smiled. "I agree."

"I'm glad." She squeezed his hand then grinned. "Just wait until you see what I've got planned for the honeymoon."

About the Author

Elley Arden is a born and bred Pennsylvanian who has lived as far west as Utah and as far north as Wisconsin. She drinks wine like it's water (a slight exaggeration), prefers a night at the ballpark to a night on the town, and believes almond English toffee is the key to happiness. Elley writes books featuring charming characters, emotional stories, and sexy romance. Visit her online at *www.elleyarden.com*.

More from This Author
(From *Running Interference* by Elley Arden)

Mmm. Mmm. Mmm. There was something about a sunny Sunday morning that put extra spring in Tanya Martin's already speedy steps. No dealing with ornery high school students and excuses about forgotten gym clothes. No football practice. Just hours to spend however she liked at her father's boxing gym.

She lifted her face to the unseasonably warm rays and wished late February in Cleveland, Ohio, always looked like this. But the heaping mounds of filthy snow lining the sidewalk reminded her winter wasn't done with them yet. She didn't care. Today was going to be a great day.

A glass door opened up ahead, and a man backed onto the sidewalk. He was so big his body loomed around the stainless steel framing, and his voice boomed when he laughed at someone inside the coffee shop. Her pace slowed as she took in his profile. Black, fitted ski jacket. Dark denim jeans that clung to his tree-trunk thighs. And a pair of designer work boots that had never set foot on a jobsite. *Not from around.* These new businesses brought in all kinds, sellouts who couldn't get through their Sundays without a double shot of something she couldn't even pronounce let alone swallow.

She put her head down and picked up her pace, wanting to pass before she was forced to say hello. She didn't want her South City neighborhood to change, and she didn't want these people getting comfortable. They weren't wanted. They weren't needed. What this place *needed* was people with a sense of loyalty and conviction—people like her parents, who both owned mom-and-pop businesses on this stretch of street. For even longer than her mother had been cooking her "almost famous" pulled-pork and holding twice-monthly Free Soup Fridays at her restaurant, Mama Mary's, her father had been taking kids off the streets and teaching them life skills with the help of boxing and martial arts at his gym. Those things were so much more important than overpriced warehouse condos and a chain coffee shop.

"Oh crap!"

The rich rumble of words came first, followed by a splash of something hot along her neck, and then an impact that had her careening toward the icy snowdrift. Her hands jutted out to break her fall, but she never hit. Instead, a crushing grip circled her right elbow and a jolt set her upright. Somehow her shoulder remained attached to its socket.

"I'm so sorry," said the deep voice again. "I … "

She looked from the work boots to the face of the trendily dressed, mammoth man, and her jaw dropped. *Cam Simmons.*

"Tanya Martin?" he asked. "Holy shit!"

Stunned into silence, she reached a hand to her neck and wiped at the droplets.

He pulled a napkin bearing the Coffee Bean logo from his pocket. "Are you okay?" He dabbed the napkin at her neck, then her chest. A little too rough. But the swipes that followed were a little too friendly.

She nodded and brushed his hand away.

How long had it been? *Five years.* Not that she'd been counting … lately. Their friendship had cooled on a barrage of texts and calls that tapered off as he got used to life away from Cleveland. Eventually the distance between them proved too great to cross. Who needed old friends when you had a shiny new multi-million-dollar NFL contract?

And that contract looked good on him, too. It had turned him into an entirely different person from the anxious, overachieving high school boy she'd spent hours with at Pop's gym. Taller and bigger, naturally, but there was also a relaxed confidence gleaming in those deep brown eyes. He didn't just want to be good; he knew he was good.

"What happened to your hair?" she blurted.

He'd had curls that rivaled hers in high school.

He palmed his nearly bald head and smiled. Somewhere angels sang. He'd always been too talented and handsome for his own good.

"I like my helmet to have a snug fit," he said. "And I was tired of messing around with skull caps. Does it look bad?"

Sly dog. Always digging for compliments, but he didn't need the ego boost. "Do you really care what I think?" Again, the last five years weighed heavy on her mind. There hadn't been so much as a Facebook like or a forwarded chain email between them. "I mean, come on. You're the Super Bowl MVP. You hardly need approval from me."

"But it would be nice." He flashed that smile again and her heart spontaneously warmed.

Disturbing. She did not want to have feelings for him after all these years. Their one night together senior year had muddied the innocent friendship, and it had taken years for her to find a neutral place, where she could hear his name, see his face, watch his games without feeling some sense of loss and hurt.

"I can't believe you're here," she said.

"I owed my mama the trip. Been promising for years. Got nothing going on until optional team activities in April, so I figured why not."

That was at least a month away. A month of running into him like this.

Shit. She backed up. "Well, it was good seeing you."

"Wait a minute." He grabbed her arm. Softer than the last time. Even through the layers of her hooded sweatshirt and long-sleeved T-shirt, she felt an unsettling tingle. "Where you running off to so fast? I'll buy you a coffee."

She glanced behind him at the gleaming monstrosity that required the leveling of two locally owned businesses to create. "No thanks. I'm not a coffee drinker. Besides, I have some ring time waiting for me."

"That's right! Pop's Gym & Ring." Deep, loud, and somehow flashy, he sounded like he'd already signed his name on a lucrative sports network announcing career. "I'm going to tag along. Say hey. Do you mind?"

She did, but if she made a big deal out of it, then she wouldn't be neutral. "Come on."

They walked the next two blocks with a safe distance between them, talking about the obvious: his Super Bowl win. It seemed safer than delving into their overly personal past. She'd never been so happy to push open the doors to the gym. Her sanctuary. She breathed in the musty smell of hard work and dedication, and exhaled her restlessness over seeing Cam.

"I'll catch ya later," she said, waving a hand at him and eyeing up the hallway that led to the locker rooms. With any luck, he'd be gone by the time she came out, and if he wasn't, maybe she'd throw on some gloves, challenge him to a few rounds, and teach him a couple things. He might be bigger and stronger, but she wasn't above hitting below the belt if need be. Hell, he deserved it.

It was always good to have a backup plan.

She ducked around a support beam and dragged her hand along the red ring ropes as she passed, smiling at a couple guys who were lifting free weights. This was still going to be a good day. Literally running into Cam Simmons was not going to change that.

Her father's office door opened and out stepped a man in a suit. Business on a Sunday? Or maybe church. That made more sense. She smiled at the man and then at her father, but her father didn't smile back. He looked stricken and pale.

"You okay, Pop?" She went to him, now highly suspicious of the well-dressed man. With all the real estate bullying that had gone on in this "up-and-coming neighborhood" over the past year, she couldn't be too careful.

"I'm fine," he said, and then he flashed an uneasy look at the man and made a gesture toward the door. "He was just leaving."

"Who is he?" She directed the question at the suit, who looked down his nose at her.

"Foreman Keller, from Great Lakes Savings and Loan, and you are?"

A banker. She lifted her chin and looked down her nose at him. "Tanya Martin, Pop's daughter." She looked at her father who was shaking his head like he wanted this conversation to end.

"Well, Tanya Martin, you might want to tell your father to pay his bills. It would save all of us time and money."

"Excuse me?" She puffed out her chest. Habit. Two older brothers, four hundred high school students, and a roster spot as a women's professional football linewoman taught her the bigger you looked the more seriously people took you.

"Stop," her father said. "It's not her concern."

"What do you mean it's not my concern?" She set her sights on the suit again. "Why are you here?"

"Just doing my job. And as long as he does his, I won't be back." He pointed at Pop. "You hear me?"

Smug *and* threatening? Not on her watch. She sort of snapped. The heels of her palms hit his lapels and knocked him back a couple feet.

"Stop!" her father said again.

"You're crazy!" The man scrambled for the door, but she followed.

"Get out and don't come back." She raised her hand for emphasis—not to hit him again—but still he flinched.

A pair of strong arms rounded her waist and halted her forward progress. A second later her back hit something hard and unforgiving, and the banker fled through the double doors.

When the arms released her, she spun around and came face-to-face with Cam. Again.

"What the hell do you think you're doing?" she spit out.

Cam's eyebrows rose. "Stopping you from getting arrested for assault."

"*Please.* I just pushed the guy. And you didn't hear how he was talking to my father." She looked around him in time to see the office door close.

What was going on? There was only one way to find out.

She raised a dismissive hand to Cam, warning him to stay away, and stalked back to the office. Her father was sitting at his desk, face in his hands. "Pop?"

He looked up, and his expression crumbled. "I'm sorry."

"For what?"

"Messin' up."

"How?" She fell to her knees and patted his thigh. "Start at the beginning."

When he exhaled, he shuddered, and her already rattled mood plummeted. Whatever it was, it was bad.

"I borrowed money to help someone out. I put the gym up as collateral, and now I'm behind on payments. I have ninety days to pay in full or they're gonna take it."

Fuck. Tanya swallowed against the lump in her throat. How the hell had this happened? She was in the gym whenever she wasn't teaching or playing football, and her brothers Terrell and Tyler were in and out too. None of them had intimate knowledge of the gym's finances, because that was Pop's thing, but somebody should've seen or sensed trouble.

He rubbed the back of her hand. "I failed everyone."

"No!" Those words didn't belong on her father's lips. He was South City's big-hearted hero. "We can fix this. We can talk to everybody in the family, and whatever you owe, we'll pull together and pay it back. It's the least we can do for everything you've done for us. How much do you owe?"

His voice muffled in his throat as he said, "Thirty thousand."

Damn it. She didn't have anywhere near that much. Neither did any of her brothers or sisters. Terrell was unemployed. Tyler's money was tied up in a messy divorce and custody battle. Tori was raising three kids on her own. And Teresa had just gone back to graduate school.

"Who'd you loan the money to?" she asked. "We'll just have to make them pay you back sooner than they expected. Then we can settle the debt."

Pop crossed his arms and hardened his expression. "Nope."

She squeezed her father's hand in an expression of sympathy and strength. "I know you don't want to call in a debt, but no friendship is worth losing the gym. Who is it?"

He looked at her, and his eyes fluttered as they rolled toward the back of his head. "I gave the money to your mother."

Tanya sat back on her heels and let his words sink in. Talk about worst-case scenario.

After a few calming breaths, she asked, "Why would Mom take $30,000 dollars from you? You haven't owed child support payments in years, and it can't be the restaurant. I live right above it, remember? It's freaking packed on weekdays."

Pop sighed. "The Diazes got an offer to sell the building to developers, so they told your mother they wouldn't be renewing her lease. She came to me panicked, and we put together an offer to buy the building ourselves."

What an unbelievable mess with her mother at the heart of it. Tanya bit back a growl. She'd been so proud of that purchase, thinking her mother had done it while standing on her own two feet. A strong, capable, independent woman. When in reality, her father had helped his ex-wife. Of course he had. His sense of obligation didn't quit. Pop Martin swooped in to save the day with no care for the trouble it would cause him.

Tanya didn't want to take sides. She'd thought she was beyond that. But in times like these, it was hard not to. The anger tossed her back seventeen years to the day he moved out of the family home. She'd been eleven, and convinced her mother was to blame.

Damn it. It just proved her theory on love and marriage. Once you loved someone enough to promise them forever, you were tied to them and their freaking problems even after forever fell apart. That's why she stayed far away from relationship strings.

"What's done is done," she said, grasping desperately at words that would help her remain neutral. "We just have to figure out a way to fix it."

There had to be an idea that would let both her parents hold onto their dreams.

She looked around, hoping for inspiration. Photographs lined the office walls, chronicling the accomplishments of the kids that had worked out in this gym. Some of them actually made it onto the few remaining college boxing teams. Her heart squeezed. This gym was so many things to so many people. Her father had even managed to bring low- and no-cost healthcare to the neighborhood in this very space by partnering with her best friend MJ's fiancé, sports medicine guru Tag Howard.

Wait! Maybe that was the answer. "What about Doc?" She jumped to her feet and pointed at the medical equipment in the partitioned corner of the office. "He's pumped a ton of cash into this place to create the training room. I bet he'd lend us more."

"No." Pop's face wrinkled. "I won't borrow any more money I can't pay back." He slapped his hands on his thighs like he'd done her whole life whenever the situation was non-negotiable. "Enough is enough. I've had a lot of time to think about this. And without any savings, my pension alone can't cover all the payments I already have. Borrowing more money would be irresponsible."

"What happened to your savings?"

Pop shrugged. "The house needed a new roof last summer."

The house where her mother lived. Tanya threw up her hands. "Unbelievable." Her father hadn't lived in that house since her parents had separated and he moved into the apartment above the gym. Sure, Tori and her kids had been living there for years, upping the responsibility Pop must've felt, but still…

How about a little independence, people? Take care of your own problems. There was a novel idea.

More deep breaths. More head shakes. "Okay," she said. "There's gotta be a way to stop this." There had to be.

Think, Tanya. Think. Something would come to her, because nobody threw a block like she did. Protection was the name of the game. They'd be prying this gym from her cold, dead hands.

A knock sounded, and she turned in time to see the door she'd forgotten to close completely swing open.

"Cam!" her father said.

"Hey," Cam said.

Great. For five years, he hadn't been anywhere to be found. Today, he was every-damn-where.

• • •

"How can I help?" Cam stepped into the office and closed the door behind him. "I couldn't help but overhear."

Pop stood. "Whatever you heard, forget about it, and get over here and give me a hug, Mr. Cam Damn Simmons." He whistled. "Super Bowl *champeen.*"

Cam hugged the little man, letting him slap him soundly on the back. He hated the circumstances he'd walked in on, but it sure felt good to be back. He'd spent so much time here as a teen, Pop had become a surrogate father to him.

"Glad to see you made it home," Pop said.

"Glad to be home."

Cam heard a scoff from someplace behind him. *Tanya.* But when he turned she was leafing through papers on her father's desk, looking uninterested in the conversation.

"Can you give my dad and me some time alone, please?" she asked without looking up.

He nodded. "Yeah. Of course." But as he backed toward the door, he made eye contact with Pop and said again, "I can help … if you let me."

Tanya glared at him. *Woo wee!* Ice cold. And it didn't get warmer until he was back in the gym.

Under the circumstances, he wasn't surprised by her reaction. He wouldn't want his dirty laundry being aired in front of anybody. But he wasn't just anybody—at least he hadn't been. That's why he'd walked in and offered to help. Apparently, five years away changed things. Something else that didn't completely surprise him. He just hadn't thought it would erase ten years of a friendship so close they were damn near family. With one exception—what had happened beneath the bleachers senior year. Thinking about it still made him smile.

They'd always been willing to go the extra mile for each other back then, and after what he'd overheard standing outside Pop's office, he wasn't going to let that change.

When Tanya had time to really talk to him, he'd get her to see he could help.

"Cam Simmons?" A short, chubby guy with moon-shaped sweat marks underneath his man-boobs stood in front of him. "No way! It's me, Goby Klinker, John-John's little brother."

"Holy crap."

They grabbed hands and bumped opposite shoulders.

"It's been forever, man," Goby said.

"I was just thinking the same thing." He looked around the gym. "Is John-John here?"

"Hell no. He's in worse shape than me. Works three jobs now because of the little ones. Hasn't been to the gym in years."

That guy had never made it to a full week of high school classes. How was he holding down three jobs? "Wait. John-John has little ones?"

"Three. Under four." Goby wrapped his hands around his neck.

Damn. "I didn't know that." He'd lost touch with the guys he used to run with too. "What about Joe and Marquis? Are they around?"

"Not around here. Joe's banned 'cause Daria thinks it's a meat market. She don't trust him."

Like Cam's ex-fiancée Sabrina hadn't trusted him. He rolled his eyes. "That sucks." Especially when it was unwarranted. "And Marquis?"

"Workin' in Atlanta. Moved about a year ago. Hear he's doing real good."

Now that was something to smile about. Marquis got out. Hopefully Cam would be saying the same thing about his mother at the end of this trip. Boston was where she belonged. With him.

"Bobby, come here!" Goby waved his hand to attract some guy's attention, and then he shifted back to Cam. "This dude's the biggest football fan. Browns, of course, but we ain't winning a Super Bowl anytime soon." He faced the room and the half-dozen guys who were lifting and practicing footwork. "Listen up, everybody! Super Bowl MVP Cam Simmons is in the house."

Cam smiled as heads turned and eyes widened. Three weeks after earning the title, and he still got a rush from it.

"What's up, gentlemen?" He raised his arms in invitation.

Something about the attention stoked his adrenaline. Always had. Like walking into school Monday morning after a big

Friday-night win. Everybody knew your name. Everybody wanted a piece of you. Powerful stuff. The kind of stuff that helped a man feel important.

He signed a few autographs and told a few "war" stories, but when Pop's office door opened and Tanya stepped out, he was too distracted to do much more than listen to the guys rattle on about football. She said something to her father, who returned to his office, and then she walked over to the punching bags and systematically went down the line pounding the hell out of each one.

"Excuse me," he said. "Gotta take care of something real quick."

He made his way through the small crowd toward Tanya, who was now whaling on a punching bag out of view from most of the gym.

"Hey," he said.

"Oh my God," she mumbled, then shot him a look, but didn't miss a beat with the bag. "You want the bag, you have to wait, Simmons. Super Bowl MVPs don't get special treatment 'round here."

He almost smiled at the exasperation in her voice.

Tanya Mary Martin. Five feet, nine inches of attitude and curves that would get a guy's head bit off if his admiration wasn't discreet. The best female basketball player East High had ever seen. And the most loyal daughter he'd ever seen. This shit with her dad was tearing her up.

"Let me help," he said.

She cut another glance at him, scornful and pitying like he was the biggest moron she'd ever seen. "He won't take your money."

"Why not?"

"Because he's proud." Boom, her fist connected with the canvas. "And we don't need your charity."

"Okay. I respect that. Fine. We'll figure something else out."

She pushed the bag into another and straightened. "*We* won't be doing anything, Cam. This is my family's problem. You are not my family."

"But I'm your friend."

She narrowed her golden eyes. "Are you? Because I thought friends stayed in touch."

Fair enough, but she could've nudged him when his silence had gone on too long. He was a busy man. But now was probably not the time to point that out, so he simply nodded. "I'm sorry about that, and I'd like to fix it. We can move on from here and not lose touch again. Deal?" He held out a hand.

She ignored his peace offering. "I've got a lot to figure out these days, so you're going to have to get in line."

Again, he almost laughed, because it had been awhile since he'd been around a woman who was so clearly not anxious to be around him. "Should I take a number?" She didn't blink at his attempt at humor. "You know, so you can call for me when it's my turn?"

"I wouldn't hold my breath, Simmons. It could take a while." She shot him a snotty smile before she turned and headed toward the hallway, then tossed over her shoulder, "Maybe like five years."

He laughed then. She'd always been a spitfire. And he had a feeling she was just getting started. He was going to be taking a lot of potshots from her over the next month.

The funny part? He kind of couldn't wait.

Praise for *Running Interference*:

"Readers need not be sports fans to appreciate the strong female lead Arden has created in Tanya. Adding to the entertainment is the sweat-inducing physicality that occurs both on the field and off."—*Library Journal*

"Arden creates a heroine worthy of the MVP title … this sports romance [is] one to root for!"—Heroes and Heartbreakers

"I love the focus on women in sports, a very underappreciated and underexposed focal point for novels. The contrast between men's and women's pro football was quite poignant. Arden, writing with her usual well-polished, light-hearted style combines this all into an unforgettable package."—Pure Jonel

"I'm a sucker for second chance romances and *Running Interference* did not disappoint. This is my first Elley Arden read and I can guarantee it won't be my last. She has a unique writing style. Simple, yet strong with fluid and easy dialogue, you can't help but dive in and not come up until you're finished."—Eat Sleep Read Reviews

For more books by Elley Arden, check out:

The Kemmons Brothers Baseball Series

Save My Soul

Change My Mind

Heal My Heart

Take Me Out

Praise for the Kemmons Brothers series:

"Nel and Gray have a lot of fun and challenging things to face . . . You will fall in love with them both . . . For a fun, sweet and very entertaining read, don't miss *Change My Mind* by Elley Arden."—Harlequin Junkie

"…Elley Arden really manages to evoke a barrage of emotions in her readers. She really has a way of creating novels that will touch you."—Texas Book Nook

"This is one of those novels that combines a multiplicity of different elements, backgrounds, and social stigmas into a single whole that will take your breath away and leave you reeling. Arden's brilliant descriptions will paint a picture you won't soon forget."—Pure Jonel

Harmony Falls Novels

Crashing the Congressman's Wedding

Battling the Best Man

Marrying the Wrong Man

Praise for the Harmony Falls series:

"The ending was my all-time favorite . . . This is definitely an AMAZING book that I recommend to all!"—Mamival's Books

"Good things come when you least expect it—at least I did with this book. I didn't expect to laugh, cry, and fall in love. But Elley Arden did those things to me, and after that short read, I think I'm coming back for more from this author."—Book Freak

Emerald Springs Legacy

Trouble Brewing

Chad's Chance